JOURNEY BEYOND
THE BURROW

RINA HEISEL

JOURNEY
BEYOND
THE BURROW

HARPER

An Imprint of HarperCollinsPublishers

Library of Congress Cataloging-in-Publication Data

Names: Heisel, Rina, author.
Title: Journey beyond the burrow / Rina Heisel.
Description: First edition. | New York : Harper, an imprint of
    HarperCollins Publishers, [2021] | Audience: Ages 8–12. | Audience:
    Grades 4–6. | Summary: "When young mouse Tobin has his baby
    brother snatched from his burrow by monstrous spiders, Tobin and his
    friends must embark on a dangerous journey deep into their forest
    home to save him, encountering new friends along the way"—
    Provided by publisher.
Identifiers: LCCN 2021000071 | ISBN 978-0-06-301603-3 (hardcover)
Subjects: CYAC: Mice—Fiction. | Forest animals—Fiction. |
    Rescues—Fiction. | Friendship—Fiction.
Classification: LCC PZ7.1.H44525 Jo 2021 | DDC [Fic]—dc23
LC record available at https://lccn.loc.gov/2021000071

Typography by Catherine Lee
Chapter opener art by Shutterstock/MicroOne
21 22 23 24 25   PC/LSCH   10 9 8 7 6 5 4 3 2 1

❖

First Edition

To Rob, Lily, and Izzy . . .
the greatest companions in any adventure

JOURNEY BEYOND
THE BURROW

one

CROUCHED IN PERFECT STILLNESS beneath a toadstool, Tobin sniffed the air. *Wet, with a faint metallic odor.*

A storm was coming, a big one. Lightning for sure. Not a good day for a mouse to venture too far from the Great Burrow. Tobin lifted his nose to the breeze again, performing the junior weather scout procedures dutifully: *Sniff the air. Search the air. Feel the air.*

He didn't even need all three steps today. The odor of rain was obvious, the clouds sat heaped in the sky like a row of giant bears, and as for feeling the air—his tan-and-black speckled fur was already clumped together from the humidity. For the third time that afternoon, Tobin rubbed his cheeks, fluffing out his fur and whiskers. After all, whiskers used properly are a fine-tuned sensory tool. Drooping whiskers can't do their job.

Speaking of which . . . Tobin sighed. He had a job to

do, and he was only halfway done. Junior weather scouts needed to deliver their reports, too.

From beneath the cover of the toadstool cap, Tobin looked toward home. The Great Burrow hunched against the earth like a giant tortoise shell: a perfectly sculpted mud clump conveniently located beside an unruly patch of blue thistle. Hidden to the untrained eye, a dozen entrances dotted the Great Burrow, carefully concealed by knots of moss and dangling roots. It was important to always use different entrances, exits, and paths while going in and out of the Great Burrow. So important, in fact, it was an official Rule of Rodentia—the survival code for all mice of the burrow.

Rule #7: A predictable path provides easy pickings for a predator.

Tobin chose an entrance he hadn't used in a while, left side—just behind a patch of crabgrass. Next, he ticked through the age-old mental checklist taught to all youngling mice:

Scan the sky. Done. No birds of prey.

Scan for ground predators. No trembling grass.

Scan the breeze. The scents are safe: clover, thistle, and honeysuckle.

The muscles in his hind legs twitched.

Go!

Tobin ran, darting a zig, then zag—enough to throw off a pouncing predator. With a final leap between blades of crabgrass, he was inside the safe confines of the Great Burrow. He blinked, waiting for his eyes to adjust to the dark inner tunnels. Only then did he tread toward his family's quarters. Memories of his morning crept into his thoughts, and his paws slowed.

Nothing but chaos waited at home. Why did his dad have to tell *all* the neighbors the pinkling was coming today? Now their den was packed with Eldermice waiting for baby news. But at least his weather scout status gave Tobin an excuse for fresh air, as he offered to make as many trips as the Eldermice wanted.

Because nothing—repeat, *nothing*—excites Eldermice like new babies and a weather report.

In fact, word about his mother going into labor spread quicker than a brushfire. That very morning, Eldermice from all corners of the burrow had begun showing up with gifts of bedding for the newborn and extra seeds and berries for Mom. And his parents, being so gracious, said they could all wait for news right there, in his family's Gathering Room.

As Tobin rounded the last bend in the tunnel before reaching home, he could hear the chatter of guests already bouncing off the mud-and-pebble-coated walls. Taking a deep breath, he prepared himself to be the center of *a lot* of attention. He wasn't wrong. "Tobin, you're back! Is the rain coming?"

"Any lightning yet?"

"Think you're getting a baby brother or sister?"

Tobin raised a paw, thankfully the dozen or so eager Eldermice grew silent (though it seemed a challenge).

"The air," Tobin began, "is getting thicker by the minute, and it's loaded with ozone, so there'll be plenty of lightning. And the clouds are growing tall, but no rain yet."

Someone called from the back of the room, "The clouds—what shape?"

Tobin fought a smile; he had a good answer for this. "The shape? Like a row of giant hunched-over bears."

Some Eldermice gasped, others looked around with concern. Lots of head shaking. Tobin couldn't help the little chuckle that shook his shoulders. *Eldermice and their drama.* It's a summer storm, not a blizzard. Now, a blizzard, that's something to worry about: food buried under snow, exit tunnels sheeting over with ice . . .

"What about the birds, Tobin?"

Tobin cleared his throat and continued. "The birds are already sheltering." He paused. Had he covered everything? Ah, one more thing. "And I have no idea if my mom is having a boy or girl."

Heads nodded and the elders seemed satisfied. Tobin rose onto his hind legs and surveyed the crowd. A narrow gap opened between furry bodies and Tobin caught a glimpse of the hallway to his room. Maybe, just maybe, he could escape for a few minutes.

Just then, someone tugged his tail. Tobin turned to see Aunt Grebba's toothy smile. Speckles of yellow pollen dust clung to her whiskers, and when she spoke, the scent of dandelion pounced off her breath.

"There's the big brother!" She clapped her front paws together and then began tickling the chin of an imaginary newborn. "A teeny-tiny little pinkling, all wrinkly, with those itsy-bitsy, curly whiskers. Are you excited Tobin?"

Tobin nodded, glancing back at his narrowing escape route. *Sludge.* The crowd was filling in.

"And your dear mother," Aunt Grebba continued. "With the burrow being so full, younger moms like yours just don't produce big batches of babies anymore. Every pinkling is so precious."

"Uh-huh," Tobin answered politely.

"Tsk-tsk." Grebba clucked her tongue. "That was a real heartbreak, last spring."

Tobin's breath caught in his snout. He snorted, swiping a paw across his muzzle.

Last spring . . .

Grebba clutched a paw to her chest. "Your poor sweet mother."

Tobin grabbed his tail and squeezed. Just nod. Think of something else. She'll think you're listening.

"Your mother was so amazing through it all, really. Always put her best face forward, truly dignified."

Tobin nodded. Remember that dead trout Wiley found yesterday? Rancid as buzzard breath.

"And now here she is, giving it yet another try." Aunt Grebba patted his head. "Such courage."

Rottenest fish ever. And that skunk still ate it . . .

"Oh dear, silly old auntie, prattling on." Aunt Grebba shook her head, snapping Tobin from his foul memories. "No need to dwell on unpleasant things."

"Suppose not," Tobin answered.

"But this weather." Aunt Grebba continued to prattle, the fur on her nose standing up. "Now there's something to talk about. Bit of a squall heading our way, eh?"

"Yeah." Tobin looked up and inched backward. "I should take my post by the window."

"Yes, yes dear," Aunt Grebba mumbled, nodding until

something caught her eye. She looked at Tobin's face as if she'd only just noticed him. "You gave a fine report, Tobin. You always do." Grebba gently took his clutched paws into hers and massaged them loose from the crushing grip on his tail. "There now, that's a bad habit, tail grabbing." Grebba then turned away to find the nearest available Eldermouse to chat up.

Mercifully, the rest of the Eldermice were absorbed in their conversations, and Tobin slid by them without so much as a pat on the head. He scurried through the corridor to his room, finally plopping onto his bed of cotton tufts.

My room. Of course, if Mom had a boy, this wouldn't be just *his room* anymore. He'd share it with the baby. Most of his friends already had brothers sharing their rooms, and sometimes they'd complain. But to Tobin, it seemed like baby brothers eventually grew into built-in playmates.

Except Wiley never complained. No, his best friend never minded sharing his room with little pups, which was good, since Wiley had four. All Tobin had was his little sister, Talia. Good news: she was fun to hang around. Bad news: she was *fun to hang around*, which meant she was also constantly surrounded by other little mouselings. Like right now, a little pink nose and tan snout began poking into Tobin's room.

"And if the pinkling is a boy," Talia was explaining to a pair of mouselings attached to her hip, "he'll share a room with Tobin, once the pinkling is a pup and grows some fur, that is. I think the baby should sleep where Tobin is, and Tobin should move his bed under the window so the little one won't get cold."

"Oh," the friends said in unison, nodding and obviously appreciating Talia's brilliance.

Tobin's whiskers twitched. "Uh, Talia?"

Ignoring him, Talia turned to the mouselings. "Since Tobin's a junior weather scout, he gets to have a window in his room. Someday I'm going to be a weather scout, too."

Tobin hopped off his bed. "Tal, I'm right here. You know you can't come in my room without asking, remember?"

Talia raised a paw, gesturing toward her companions. "But we have company, and I'm just giving a tour."

Her friends giggled. Like a moonbeam surrounded by moths, Talia sat firmly planted in the center of the mouseling universe.

Tobin's fur bristled. "You know you guys don't count as *company*. Mom and Dad said you can't come in here without asking, and since they're pretty busy in their own room, I'll tell you all for them. Get. Out."

Talia's friends' eyes grew to the size of blueberries. She glanced over her shoulder. "Meet you guys back in my room, okay?" The mouselings ducked out, and Talia stepped closer to Tobin. "Are you nervous about the baby?"

Tobin's ears flattened. "What?"

Talia scratched her chin, like she always did when trying to think of just the right words. "It's just," she began, "you're acting a little crabbier than normal, and I know I was scared at first when Dad said the baby was coming today because of what happened last time, so if you—"

"Stop." A fissure of nerves erupted: fear, sadness . . . annoyance. Tobin's fur bristled. "I don't want to talk about the baby and not because I'm scared." Tobin felt his lip curl as he spoke, though he didn't mean to actually snarl. "I've had to talk about baby stuff all day while you got to hang out and play with your friends. I've done two weather reports, checked on guests, and now I just want to have a little break. Maybe be alone for a minute?" Tobin tapped a hind paw, trying to funnel some of his annoyance away, into the floor beneath him. "So sorry if that makes me crabby."

"It sounds like you need a nap." Talia spun around,

her tail a whisker's-breadth away from smacking Tobin in the face. She only came up to his shoulder in height, but her bravado was bear-sized. As she walked back into her room, he overheard her friends: "You were just trying to be nice," and "Maybe he's a big deal to the junior weather scouts, but he really needs to work on his manners."

For the second time in a minute, Tobin's fur bristled. He stuck his head into the hallway. "You want manners? Fine. *Please* remember I'm awful, so *please* don't try coming in here anymore, *thank you very much*."

A trio of giggling mouselings was all he got for his trouble.

Tobin rubbed his paws over his fur, smoothing his tan-and-black-speckled coat into place. Would the new baby have black-tipped fur like him? Or all tan, like Talia? Speckles made for great camouflage, but—

Stop.

No thinking this way. No getting hopes up. Not for fur color, not for a brother or sister, nothing.

A gust of wind whipped through his window and tickled his whiskers. The storm. Any other day and he'd be watching that storm roll in with Wiley. Tobin's ear cocked.

Maybe he still could?

If he could just get Wiley up here. Wiley's family lived

below, in the burrow caverns. Almost directly below.

He glanced toward his door as the voices of Eldermice filled his ears. Crowds. Questions. Grebba.

Tobin winced. No way out except . . .

He looked up. He wasn't supposed to use his walnut-sized window as an exit. *Ever.* But maybe this one time, just to get Wiley. They could do weather reports together. Four eyes watching the weather beats two, right?

And if there was ever a time Mom and Dad wouldn't catch on . . .

Tobin pounced onto the dirt wall and scaled it up to the window. The small, circular opening was held fast in place with packed tree bark, pebbles, and river clay, hidden from the outside world by strategically hanging roots. When he reached his two front paws through, a few small stones clattered to the floor. No big deal. He could patch that later. He poked his head outside, his nose pushing through the curtain of roots. He squeezed his front side through, but when he wriggled his rear end out, a clump of packed mud fell from the window frame, hitting his bedroom floor with a hard *SPLUT.* He heard a pebble skitter across his floor, followed by a voice.

"Tobin! What are you doing?"

Sludge.

two

WITH CLAWS DIGGING INTO the outer wall, Tobin poked his head back inside.

Talia, her mouth hanging open like a trout, stood in the middle of his room. At least she was alone.

"Tobin, you are in so, *so* much trouble."

The words tumbled from his mouth. "Please don't tell anyone!"

She scurried beneath the windowsill. "What are you doing?"

"I'm just going to see Wiley. It's no big deal."

"Wait, what?" The excited spark in Talia's eyes fizzled. "You told me you needed a break. You wanted to be alone." Her ears drooped. "You really don't like me."

"What? No." Tobin shook his head. *How do I say this?* "Tal, I like hanging out with you, just not when you have a bunch of friends over. I like when it's just us. But right now, all your friends are over, so I'm going to visit Wiley. He's a weather scout, too, after all."

Talia's ears lifted. "So you have someone to do reports with?"

Tobin nodded. "Exactly. Now, I really need to go."

Talia looked at the crumbled mess on the floor. "You'll be grounded for wrecking that window."

"Are you gonna tell on me or what?"

"I won't," Talia said, the shimmer returning to her eyes like she'd just solved a riddle. "I won't tell anyone *if* you take me to the creek tomorrow—just us."

A smile crinkled Tobin's cheeks. "I'll take you to the creek."

"Good. But don't be gone too long, because—"

"I know, I know. The baby's coming." Tobin shimmied down the outer wall, careful to stay beneath the dangling camouflage. His dad always compared the burrow to an anthill; the dirt mound above ground was only a hint of the massive tunnel system running beneath. That's where Wiley lived. His family was one of the Great Burrow's founding families, and their quarters below were spacious but dug deep into the earth. Tobin preferred having a room with a breeze. He scaled down to a lower burrow entrance and ducked inside. Taking the tunnels downward, he felt the dirt floors damp beneath his paws, and the scent of clay and earthworms grew stronger.

As he neared his friend's quarters, a familiar voice echoed off the tunnel walls—Wiley's mom. "You will not keep that caterpillar in here—please return it where you found it."

"But Mom, please?"

Tobin peeked around the entryway.

Wiley stood wobbling on his hind legs, clutching a squirming, striped caterpillar that dangled nearly to the ground. "But it's going to rain any minute. Can we just keep him till tomorrow?"

"No, Wiley, the caterpillar will be fine outside." Wiley's mom shook her head, and then she noticed Tobin in the doorway. Smiling, she waved him in. "Oh look, Tobin's here. Any baby news?"

"Not yet," Tobin answered, walking inside the cozy den. It was crammed with treasures the older pups dragged home. A dried-out clover hung on the wall, above a hollowed-out walnut shell Wiley had found, which they used as a seed bin. In the corner, the two youngest mouse pups napped in the husk of a gourd.

"You're here just in time, Tobin." She nodded toward Wiley. "He was about to take this caterpillar back outside. Perhaps you could help him."

"But—" Wiley started.

"Stop," she said firmly. Swishing her tail forward, she pointed from Wiley to Tobin. "While the two of you are outside, grab some dandelion sprouts for Tobin's mom. Fresh ones."

Wiley's ears flattened to his head. The left one sported a fresh red scab. "Fine. I'll grab some dandelion, but maybe we could . . ."

One of the pups squeaked from inside the hollowed gourd. Wiley's mom scurried over, gently lifting the squeaking pup by the scruff of its neck. She lay down, nestling the fuzz-covered babe beside her. When she spoke again, her voice was hushed. "Tobin, please tell your mom I'd have loved to stop by today, but . . . well, things are just a little hectic around here."

"I'll tell her," Tobin said.

Wiley jerked his chin toward the door. "At least we have an excuse to go outside."

Nothing sounded better.

As they stepped into the burrow tunnels, Tobin nearly ran into Wiley's little brother Smudge.

Smudge's mouth gaped open, accentuating the dark gray streak running from his forehead to the tip of his nose. "What is that?"

"Oh, this?" Wiley shrugged. "Just a caterpillar. I was going to go throw it back outside."

"Wait!" Smudge reached out a paw, patting the fuzz-covered larva. "Can I have it?"

"Hmm." Wiley cocked his head. "I guess. Just make sure not to bother Mom with it. She's getting the pups to sleep. Take it back to our room. Oh, and there's milkweed by my bed."

Smudge nodded enthusiastically. If the mouseling was suspicious of Wiley's generosity, he didn't show it. Wiley draped the caterpillar over Smudge's shoulders, and the younger mouse waddled away. Tobin slapped a paw over his muzzle to keep from laughing.

A satisfied smile spread across Wiley's face. "We should go."

"Yeah." Tobin laughed as his claws gripped the tunnel floor. "Race you."

Wiley flicked his tail. "You're on."

Tobin bolted. Paws pounding the lumpy floor, they raced down the tunnel away from Wiley's, like they had a hundred times before. *Lean left, lean right.* Tobin built speed until his paws barely grazed the floor. Swerving past a few startled mice, they burst out an exit hole, plowing into the nearest shrub.

This was poor usage of the Rules.

"One of these days," Tobin panted, "there'll be a badger sitting here waiting for us."

Wiley leaned against a low, scraggly branch, his dark-brown head and paws blending perfectly with the wood. "No way."

"No way, huh?" Tobin cocked his head. "Kind of like *no way* that blue jay was going to chase you down yesterday?"

"That's different." Wiley rubbed a paw over his newly scabbed ear.

"Really?" Tobin said, peeking out from the shelter of the shrub. Deeming it safe, he scurried to a patch of freshly sprouted dandelion. "How's your ear today?"

Wiley pounced from his spot beneath the bough. "It only hurts if I touch it. Mom got a little mad. Dad just said he knew I'd never keep a perfect set of ears. At least that bird only got the tip."

Tobin nodded. "And you kept the acorn."

"Of course!" Wiley pounced on the yellow-puffed weed growing beside Tobin's. "It was delicious."

Tobin chomped through a dandelion stem and nibbled off some leaves, too. One perk of gathering fresh stems for Mom was snacking a little himself, too. Something tickled his nose, and he rubbed a paw over his face. It came away wet with dew. "We'd better hurry up."

In the distance, a crack of thunder rolled through the sky. For a moment the whole forest was still, as if bracing for what came next.

Tobin scooped up his heap of clippings in his paws. "I'd say we have enough."

Wiley nodded silently, grabbing his pile, too.

Cramming the pieces in his mouth, Tobin ran toward the burrow entrance, craning his neck to keep the cuttings from tangling his paws. Even so, he almost tripped when he saw Talia waiting at the burrow entrance, sitting under a clump of moss.

"Wudda look at dat?" Wiley muttered through his veggie-filled jaws.

Tobin spit the bundle from his mouth. "How'd you find us, pipsqueak?"

Her face puckered like she'd eaten a bad berry. "Don't call me that. Wiley's mom sent me this way."

"Why?" Tobin raised a brow.

Sour face gone, Talia bounced from paw to paw.

"Because I had to get you. It's Mom, she had the baby!"

Tobin's stomach flipped. "What?"

"The pinkling!" Talia clapped her paws. "It's here! We have to go."

"It's here." Tobin felt like a million little pebbles were sloughing off his back. A smile crossed his muzzle. "And it's healthy?"

"Yes," Talia squealed. "It came really fast, probably when you were sneaking out."

Wiley's ears flicked straight up. "You snuck out?"

"Oh." Tobin's nose twitched. "Did I not mention that?"

Talia continued. "Dad said once I find you, we can go in and see Mom and the baby." She raised a paw. "Don't worry, I told him you were just out checking the weather again, this time with Wiley."

A sudden crack of thunder sent Tobin's toes curling into the dirt. Talia's eyes went wide as moons.

"Storm's almost here." Wiley practically shook with excitement.

"We can watch from my window," said Tobin.

"Or"—Wiley raised a furry brow—"you know what we could do?"

Tobin flattened an ear. *Oh no . . .*

Wiley clapped his paws together. "I heard the

Eldermice say that sometimes, when the air is damp before a storm—like today—the sky turns green before the rain comes. Green! We should check it out from Lookout Landing."

Talia looked at Wiley like he'd sprouted a second tail. "Hello, did you hear what I said? My mom just had her baby. I'm supposed to find Tobin and go home."

"Just a really quick look." Wiley stretched out his front legs, his head dipping low, round eyes staring up at Talia. "Please? Even the Eldermice are saying this could be the storm of the century—a once-in-a-lifetime chance."

Talia sat back on her hind legs and crossed her front paws.

"Ah, sludge." Wiley's eyes rolled and his tail flopped back and forth. "Don't be such a tadpole, Talia."

Her cheek fur puffed. "I'm *not* a baby!"

"Quiet a sec." Tobin raised a paw just as another clap of thunder cracked the air. A thrill of joy ran through him. *Mom's fine. The baby's fine. Now—the storm of the century awaits.* Outside, a roar of wind rustled the trees. Tobin sniffed. The downpour was close. If they hurried, maybe they could see both? "Lookout Landing's a pretty quick trip up the tunnel from our den."

Wiley pumped his paw in the air. "Yes!"

"How about this?" Tobin directed his stare at Talia. "We run up and meet the baby, then ask if we can go to Wiley's to tell his mom the news." Now Tobin shifted his gaze to Wiley. "Except maybe on the way to Wiley's den, we take a quick detour and peek out at Lookout Landing."

Talia pointed a tiny claw at Tobin. "You always let Wiley get you into trouble."

"Wiley, would you give us a sec?" Tobin jerked his head toward the upward-winding tunnel.

His friend's nose twitched impatiently, but Wiley turned, scooped up his dandelion pickings, and scampered up the curvy passageway.

"Listen, Tal." Tobin turned to Talia once they were alone. "The baby is okay! Mom is okay! We all want to be full-fledged weather scouts someday, right? Observing a real green sky can't hurt."

Talia traced circles in the dirt with her paw as she considered his words. "But I don't like sneaking. Mom would want to know if we went up there, right?"

"Normally, yes." Tobin waved a paw, trying to sound as nonchalant as possible. "But Mom's got her paws full, right? New pinkling! Getting out of her fur for a few minutes would probably be a good thing."

"All right," Talia conceded. "It would be amazing to see the storm." Her eyes brightened, flickering with happiness. "But first—we meet the baby!"

"Yes, we do." Tobin whipped his tail and called up to Wiley. "Let's head up!"

three

ON THIS TRIP BACK to his den, Tobin's paws felt especially light, despite the load of fresh dandelion trimmings he carried in his mouth. Amazing how much things had changed since morning. Now Tobin practically floated through the Gathering Room, returning the smiles of all the Eldermice who offered their congratulations. This time, the Eldermice let him easily pass by, and Tobin was very grateful. After all, he had a baby to meet! Of course, Tobin ducked to avoid eye contact with Aunt Grebba, knowing she could accidentally wilt daisies with her words no matter the occasion.

Tobin, Talia, and Wiley trod down the hall to his parents' room. His uncle Derry sat crouched in the entrance like a doorkeeper, ensuring boisterous visitors remained out in the Gathering Room; tranquil visitors only beyond this point. Uncle Derry smiled at the sight of Tobin, and his grin widened farther upon noticing Talia and Wiley trailing right behind.

"There you are," Derry said, his voice hushed. "Ah . . ." He nodded his big brown head. "Seems you were weather watching *and* picking some fresh greens."

Reaching up with his paw, Tobin grabbed the clutch of cuttings from his jaws and set it beside the entryway. "Just trying to be helpful," he replied in a hushed voice. "Why are we whispering, Uncle?"

"Because your parents and the babe have all fallen asleep," he answered. "You know they had a long night."

"Oh no," Talia replied, her voice dripping with disappointment.

The warm heat of embarrassment pooled in Tobin's cheeks and rose up into his ears. Because he'd snuck out with Wiley, they'd have to wait to meet the baby.

"Now, hang on there," Uncle Derry said, the lilt in his voice indicating maybe all was not lost. "No need for the sad faces. If you're quiet—which I know you scouts can be—you can go take a peek at your new family member."

Talia straightened, and even her whiskers perked up. "Oh, we can be quiet, promise."

"Then I think your folks would love for you to have a

look. Go on." Uncle Derry stepped aside.

Tobin smiled and nodded, setting his dandelion greens inside the room for his mom to enjoy later. A peek was better than nothing! His excitement bubbled back up, and as he led the procession into his parents' quarters, his toes tingled with every step. As he neared his mother, his nose caught the sweet scent of milk. His eyes widened upon seeing the tiny form of the pinkling, no bigger than a pumpkin seed, pressed up against his mother's silvery gray fur.

As Talia wriggled in beside him, Tobin knew exactly when her eyes fixed on the new baby, because she was suddenly perfectly still.

Tobin leaned over to her. "How were we ever that small?"

Talia smiled back, just shrugging. As she looked back at the pinkling, her eyes widened. "Oh, Tobin, look."

The pinkling stretched a bit, kicking out its tiny back legs before snuggling up close again. Its tiny tail curled around itself in sleep, and Tobin gasped. The baby's tail was already a dark gray.

"Would you look at that." Wiley leaned in closer.

"Ahem." Uncle Derry quietly cleared his throat from the doorway.

"I think our time's up," Tobin noted.

Talia nodded, leaning in for one last look and sniff. "Like milk and dandelions."

"Yeah," Tobin agreed. "C'mon, we better head out."

"Don't forget." Wiley smiled a sneaky grin. "We have another stop to make."

As the three mice scooted past Uncle Derry, Tobin had a thought. "Here, into my room, quick."

Wiley and Talia followed him, and Wiley's stare went right to the window, then to the scattering of pebbles on the ground. "Oh yeah, I see what you did now."

Tobin flicked his tail. "Do you know how many questions those Eldermice will have for us in the Gathering Room? Sure, they let us pass through on the way to meet the pinkling. But on the way out? Oh no. They'll have questions—about a hundred of them! We can't risk going back through a second time."

Tobin watched as the realization dawned on Wiley's and Talia's faces.

"We'll be stuck forever," Wiley whispered.

"Exactly." Tobin scurried over to the window. "But since I've gotta fix this window anyway, we may as well use it one more time." Tobin scaled the wall, then looked back to Talia and Wiley. "So, there's a breezeway vent just a quick climb above us. It should be wide enough that we can reenter the burrow and head up the main tunnel to Lookout Landing."

A smile slowly sprouted across Wiley's muzzle. "I like the way you think."

Talia bounced nervously from paw to paw. "The window?" Talia looked to the battered frame of the opening, then back to Tobin. "It's just, we're not supposed to use the window. I know you have before, but . . ."

Tobin narrowed his eyes ever so slightly, trying to silently remind her of their prior conversation. "Yes, Tal. Out the window. To see the storm. Weather scouts. Any of this ring a bell?"

Talia wrung her paws together, and Tobin could feel his patience dwindle. "Okay," he said. "Wiley, I think Talia would rather stay here, so we can just go, and—"

"Wait." Talia sat up and steadied herself. "So, you really think if I see this unusual sky it'll help me get into the weather scouts?"

A mixture of pride and relief swept through Tobin. Pride in Talia for mustering her courage, and relief that if she came, she definitely would *not* tell on them. "For sure! I bet no other mice in your brood group will see this storm from Lookout Landing."

Talia's head bobbed in quick nods, like she was eager

27

to convince herself, too. "I suppose we can't even ask Mom and Dad's permission right now anyway. Just promise we'll be fast?"

"Promise." Tobin nodded. "And we'll get this window all patched up before anyone notices we're gone."

Wiley sniffed the air. "The storm's scent is strong; we need to move."

Talia agreed. "Okay."

"Follow me, stay close," Tobin instructed. He poked his head out the window and sniffed. The smells of the forest were amplified by the plopping raindrops, but so far, everything was safe. They could move.

Tobin slid the rest of his body out his window, clinging to the cobbled surface of the Great Burrow. Looking left and upward, he could see the pebbled ridge that marked a breezeway—their entrance. Tobin shivered as a gust of wind rippled the fur along his back, and he gripped the wall harder. Okay, so severe-weather climbing might present some new challenges. The little daylight that remained broke through the blowing canopy of vines and cast shadows that danced and skipped along the burrow wall. This would be a short climb, but it required some care.

Tobin glanced back to his companions. "Follow my

pawholds, okay? I'll find good places to grip. Talia, stay right on my tail."

They nodded back at him, and Tobin made his first move. *Reach, find hold, pull up.* Tobin repeated this technique, relying on his sense of touch instead of sight, since the bouncing shadows were enough to deceive his vision. A quick glance up determined he was on target, and the sounds of claws on clay below assured him that Talia and Wiley were close behind.

One more stretch and grab, and Tobin's paw hit the ledge of the breezeway. Only a narrow slit in the wall, it was just wide enough for fresh air to pass into the Great Burrow. Tobin smiled. *Just wide enough for three junior-sized mice to squeeze through.*

Tobin cocked his head, angling his ear directly below the opening. He called over his shoulder, "It's all clear. Let's head in."

Tobin reached his paws into the crevice and pulled himself through, dropping down into a main corridor. He slid to the side, leaving room for Talia to fall in beside him, followed by Wiley.

Wiley leaned back on his haunches and clapped his front paws, his whiskers quivering with excitement. "Better hightail it before we miss the show," he said as he leaped forward, scurrying around the bending tunnel before Tobin could even answer.

Tobin eyed his sister. "Stay close to me up there, okay?"

She lifted her chin. Tobin saw the "I'm not a baby" speech ready to fly. He quickly raised a paw. "I'm not worried about *you*, Tal. Think about it: rain, lightning, danger—and Wiley."

The whites flashed around the dark centers of her eyes. "We'd better go."

Running up the cobbled tunnel to Lookout Landing, Tobin couldn't help but notice they were the only mice heading up—not down. He studiously avoided eye contact with any mouse they passed. No questions meant no mouse telling them to turn around. Rounding one final curve, he finally saw Wiley crouching beneath a shaft. When Tobin and Talia reached him, they looked up. The narrow passageway, wide enough for a single mouse, led skyward.

"See you topside," said Wiley. He sprang into the shaft and shimmied upward. Tobin nodded to Talia, then squatted, set, and jumped.

As soon as Tobin entered the tunnel, he could feel gusts of air brush the tips of his ears. He quickly ascended the narrow tunnel, pushing himself into the open air of Lookout Landing.

WHOOSH!

Wind slapped his face like a splash of water. The thickly knit shrubs atop the Great Burrow usually acted like a weather barrier, but today the gusts spun the spindly branches in circles. Dust and pebbles whirled like little tornadoes.

Tobin looked to Wiley, who sat beside the entrance.

The wind whipped Wiley's whiskers back and forth across his face. "Can you believe this?"

Tobin scurried beside his friend, hunkering beneath some woven twigs. Like a hawk hovering in the air, thick black clouds hung above the canopy of trees. But in between the clouds, small patches of sickly green sky broke through.

Wiley gasped. "A green sky."

A shiver danced down Tobin's spine. "It looks . . . angry," he shouted as the wind threatened to drown out his words. He looked back to the shaft. Was Talia coming? She had to see this.

Wiley bounced from paw to paw. "Can you believe how dark it is? It's barely midday!"

Tobin shook his head. From the corner of his eye he saw a pink nose cautiously sniffing the whirling air. Tobin raised his voice again. "C'mon Tal, it's windy but not that wet. There's a genuine green sky."

31

Talia peeked out, flinching as the first gust whipped past her ears. Then she darted beside him, and he smiled and nudged her shoulder. "Pretty brave for a mouseling."

Her forehead smoothed a little. "I'm no skittish fish."

"Let's head over to the ledge," said Wiley. "We can see the whole storm from there without all this bramble in the way."

And there it was. Whenever Wiley was involved, plans tended to shift and change directions like a bat flitting after bugs in the night sky. But this was too much. It was one thing taking risks just him and Wiley, but with Talia, too . . .

Rule #13: Heed the whispered warnings of weather; ignoring its clues will spell your doom.

A raindrop fell. Then another. A steady shower began. "Not today, Wiley. Rule Thirteen! Besides, I promised Talia we'd go in when it really started raining."

"Seriously?" Wiley cocked his head. "We just got out here."

"Wind *and* rain? No way." Tobin's nose twitched. "I can't smell or hear a thing. And neither can you. We should head down."

"Fine, go in and babysit." Wiley squinted, peering through the rain. "No way predators are out in this rain.

I'm going to take a look. I'll let you know how awesome the view was."

"Wait," Tobin said, but it was too late. Wiley skittered out to the ledge, the pounding of the raindrops doing little to dampen his enthusiasm.

"He's hawk bait out there," Talia said.

"I know," Tobin answered. "Hop back into the shaft, okay? I need to—"

Talia gasped. "What is he doing?"

One branch jutted out from the ledge. Naturally Wiley was creeping onto it.

"He's a loon," Tobin whispered.

Thunder rumbled. Lightning ripped the sky like eagle talons.

"We should go in now!" Talia said.

CRACK!

The world went blindingly white. Bolts of lightning splintered in every direction. From a distance, Tobin heard a pop and a sizzle, followed by the sounds of wood snapping. Tobin blinked wildly, his vision clearing just in time to see the canopy of a cottonwood tree falling toward them.

Throwing a paw around his sister, Tobin shoved them both as deep into the bramble as he could. The world shook as the cottonwood crashed to the forest floor. Then all was still and silent, minus the pounding of the rain. Tobin peeked out from his hiding place and saw the timber had landed a deer's leap away from the burrow.

Then his gaze landed on the branch where Wiley had been; the limb bobbed empty in the wind. "Wiley," Tobin gasped.

His heart raced like a trapped hummingbird. "Go inside, Tal. Wait at the bottom of the shaft."

She shook her head. "Where are you going?"

"Just get inside, *please*." Tobin looked to the ledge. "I'll be right behind you."

"Okay," she agreed, hopping into the shaft, but not all the way down—she peeked out to watch.

"Good enough," Tobin muttered.

Crouching low, he crept toward the ledge. Mud exploded around him as raindrops pelted the soil. He tried sniffing for Wiley, but all he could smell was earth and rain.

"Wiley!" he called. The Rules howled in every fiber of his being: *danger!*

Fighting his instinct to flee, Tobin pushed ahead, one step at a time. He crept until he could peer over the very brim of the burrow. Cascading water, splashing mud, and the last throes of lightning smeared his vision. The search was hopeless.

Until something bizarre caught his eye.

A purple violet bounced merrily below, directly beneath him. He stared at the flower until he could make out Wiley standing near the foot of the burrow, signaling with the bloom that he was all right. Tobin released his breath in relief and waved back. Wiley instantly dropped the violet and darted inside a burrow entrance far below them.

Tobin pulled his claws from the muddy ledge and slogged his way back to the shaft.

"Did you find him?" Talia was peeking over his shoulder.

"He's fine. Move down so I can get in."

They slid back into the burrow, the sounds of the storm now muffled by the earthen wall. Tobin could hear his heart pounding in his ears. He shook what mud he could off his coat, but it stuck like clay.

Talia clucked her tongue. "You are a total mess."

Tobin tucked his head, examining the layers of mud clumps on his belly. "Ugh, this is pretty bad." He whipped his head up, and his mind spun a bit. That feeling, combined with the nerves, and what a mess he was, set him to giggling.

Talia slapped her tail to the ground. "You think this

is *funny*? This wasn't a 'quick peek at the clouds.' This was dangerous!"

"I know." Tobin shook his head, though he didn't succeed in shaking the grin from his muzzle. "Wiley probably shouldn't have gone out that far."

"Probably?"

"Let's just find him and get home." Tobin set off down the tunnel. "Did you see the lightning strike that tree? And how close it landed to the burrow? I wonder if anyone else saw it."

"I bet they felt it," Talia answered.

"Huh." Tobin nodded. As he pondered the thought, he didn't notice the lump of mud tottering toward him.

"Hey, Tobin!" called the mud lump in a voice that sounded a lot like Wiley's. "I thought that tree was gonna land right on us."

A sigh of relief escaped Tobin, and a small smile sprouted on Talia's muzzle.

"See, Tal?" Tobin nudged her shoulder. "We can be fun."

"I suppose," she said, looking at Wiley. "Will your mom let you in your quarters like that?"

He shrugged. "She's seen worse."

"You could wash off over there." Talia pointed to a corridor. It was a burrow breezeway, a narrow corridor with a window at the end, letting fresh air flow into the burrow. Thanks to the rain, a little waterfall cascaded over the small window. Perfect for a quick shower.

Wiley gave an approving nod. "I think our moms would rather us be wet than mud-caked."

Tobin scratched at his own muck-covered hide. "Agreed." He scurried into the corridor, Wiley on his tail. The dirt floor of the breezeway itself was mushy from rivulets of water seeping inside, but if they walked carefully along the sides of the tunnel, they could avoid most of the muck. Reaching into the opening, they grabbed pawfuls of water and began scrubbing their fur.

"This was a good idea," said Wiley.

"Yeah, Talia's pretty clever. I just wish she wouldn't worry about every little thing sometimes."

Wiley shrugged. "She's still little. Little mice do that."

Of course, Wiley had a pawful of littles to deal with at home, so Tobin supposed he was an expert.

But, as if Talia wanted to prove his point, her worried voice rang through the corridor. "Tobin, come here. Hurry!"

"See?" said Tobin. Fur sopping wet and still half caked in mud, Tobin shuffled into the tunnel. "What?"

Talia sprang to his side. "There are really weird noises coming from down that tunnel." She clutched her tail, her voice rising till she sounded like a chickadee. "I think I heard a scream!"

"A scream?" Tobin peered down the tunnel. Talia might exaggerate some things, but he doubted she'd mistake a scream for anything but that. "Stay here."

Tobin took a step down the tunnel, ears and whiskers pricked. He padded silently through the passageway until it came to a sharp corner. Lowering his head, he leaned his ear against the wall. A strange sound like scuttling, clicking footsteps tapped through the tunnel. Tobin's neck fur spiked.

That sound . . .

It didn't belong in the burrow.

"What's happening?" Wiley hollered.

Tobin held up his paw—*Shhhh*. He paused a moment. While Wiley no longer called out, Tobin could hear his and Talia's pawsteps coming his way.

Tobin whipped his tail twice, and the pawsteps ceased. Hoping they wouldn't follow him any farther, Tobin stepped around the corner.

The long tunnel he expected to see was half caved in. Tobin squinted; the passageway wasn't filled in with dirt or clay. No, whatever this was—it squirmed. It was alive.

four

THE NEXT THING TOBIN noticed was the horrible odor. It smacked his nose; it was rancid, sharp. Beyond worse than decay. His body braced to run, but his mind stilled his feet. *Something is in your home. Look and learn—quickly.*

With a paw over his snout, Tobin took a trembling, three-legged hop toward the bulk. What kind of cave-in smelled bad and moved? He focused on the blackish mound until a shape began to form before him.

A creature, *a big one*, was trying to shove its way through the tunnel. Tobin's throat ran dry as he made out a tiny nub of a head resting on a giant black body. He only figured it was a head because of the quivering patch of blood-red eyes—at least a dozen of them. Jutting from beneath the head was a set of pincers. Like a pair of jagged crescent moons, the pincers flexed open and closed as the creature struggled forward.

Muscles quivering, Tobin stepped back just as the creature wiggled a long, dark appendage free from under its body. *A leg?* Segmented and insect-like, the limb clicked as its armor-plated sections stretched out. The leg scraped along the tunnel wall, then stopped. It suddenly stabbed down, driving its wicked tip deep into the packed dirt.

Tobin jumped backward, whiskers and ears pricked to full attention. He watched another leg unfurl from beneath the beast. And another. The limbs clawed at the walls and floor, searching out footholds so it could move—move closer to him.

Tobin let his stare linger a moment longer until it became painfully clear what he was looking at.

A spider!

Like no spider he'd ever seen before.

With its front four legs finding a grip, the beast yanked itself forward.

Tobin had seen enough. He bolted back around the corner, his paws skidding to a stop beside Talia and Wiley. Before he could utter a word, Talia's nose twitched at the stench stuck to his coat. Her fur puffed. Wiley crouched and growled.

"It's a spider, I think. Nastiest thing I've ever seen."
Tobin looked over his shoulder. A gnarled leg poked
around the bend in the corridor. "We need to go back to
the breezeway where we washed off. Move!"

"That's a sp-sp-spider?" Talia took a step back toward
the corridor.

Wiley remained frozen; a rumble grew in his chest.
His tail whipped wildly from side to side.

Tobin knew the cues. The signs were laid out in the
Rules: fight or flight. Talia readied for flight, Wiley for
a fight.

But fight a monster spider? Not a chance.

Tobin stepped in front of his friend, breaking Wiley's
gaze. "Trust me, we have to hide. Whatever you're
thinking—"

Wiley looked past Tobin, his friend's eyes doubling in
size. All pink drained from Wiley's nose. Dreading what
he was about to see, Tobin turned.

Long, black legs reached around the bend, each seeming to be on its own mission of exploration, bending and
flexing what seemed like countless joints.

"*That* is why we need get inside the corridor," Tobin
hissed.

"Yup." Wiley turned and scrambled.

Tobin nudged Talia's shoulder with his head. "Let's move!"

Talia stepped back slowly, her breath coming in shallow gasps. "Wait, I think I hear something else."

"We've gotta go, Tal!" Tobin poked his snout into her side, spinning her backward.

They scurried down the tunnel, stopping at the waterlogged corridor. Throwing one quick look over his shoulder before diving in, Tobin saw the crimson eyes. The brute rounded the bend and was scraping its way in their direction.

"Cripes!" Talia poked her head out beneath his.

"Scoot in," Tobin whispered, shuffling all way to the rear of the soggy passage. "Stay close to the dripping water. Wriggle into the mud and hold still."

"Should we run?" Wiley's eyes traced the dripping water from the ceiling above to the small breeze hole. "Bet we could claw through that pretty fast."

Tobin shook his head. "I don't think it can get us in here; it's barely fitting through the main tunnels. But if it tries, we'll bolt."

Wiley nodded, and they shimmied deep into the muck, huddled at the far end of the corridor. Rivulets of rainwater dripped on their foreheads. Tobin blinked it away, but didn't dare move another muscle. The spider was getting close.

Click, click, click, click—scrape.

The first probing leg stepped into view. Tobin watched as the massive spider pulled through the tunnel. He shivered. One of the spider's legs lost its grip, catching on the corridor entrance. Tobin didn't breathe. The sharp tip of the appendage reached into the shaft, feeling the sides and ceiling. It stretched inside, hovering over Tobin's head like a fang. He could count the bristly hairs poking out between joints. A trickle of water dripped and spattered the leg, and it recoiled, banging one of its many knees on the ceiling.

This spider, it seemed, wasn't interested in a wet passageway.

Up to his chest in mud, Tobin finally exhaled. He wanted to clamp his eyes shut and wait for the freakish spider to pass, but he forced himself to watch.

Rule #22: Study your enemies, for all creatures have a weakness.

Another leg crossed his view, then finally, the lump of its head. Rows of red eyes quivered above a set of pincerlike fangs. Did the spider see them, hunkered in the mud? If it did, would it care? It seemed possessed, determined to get through the tunnel.

Tobin lost sight of its face (if he could even call it a face) as it pressed forward, giving way to its disk-shaped midsection. The creature's legs sprouted from its middle, rippling front to back as the beast scuttled forward. Finally, the spider's rear section came into sight. A strange, wheezing rasp sounded from this final, pear-shaped segment of spider. And at the very end of its bulbous back end, two fingerlike digits curved upward. On a normal spider, Tobin knew these small digits were called spinnerets—and they made the webs the spiders spun. But nothing about this spider was normal, including its spinnerets, which appeared to be clutching a tiny lump of webbing, much like a cocoon.

Tobin cocked his head to get a better look as the giant arachnid passed by. His sudden movement earned a quick elbow in the shoulder from Talia, so he remained still until the arachnid was fully out of view.

Slowly pulling himself up from the mud, he whispered, "Stay here." Tobin crept to the rim of the corridor, peeking out to get a closer look. He got a clear view of the webbed bundle carried on the spider's backside. What could that be? It looked so out of place; it was soft and silky, and cradled so delicately by an eight-legged monster. Wiley crept up alongside him, but Tobin never took his eyes off the cocoon.

The sack of webbing twitched.

Now Tobin stepped fully out into the tunnel. There was *something* in that sack. He took a few cautious steps after the spider. Could it be an egg sack, full of mini monster spiders? No, why would a spider risk carrying its babies on a hunting trip?

Whatever was in that bundle was alive, though too small to be a mouse.

Unless . . .

The thought made his stomach flip. His breath caught in his throat. He looked to Wiley and whispered the quietest whisper he could manage. "Did you see the websack?"

Wiley nodded.

A breeze blew down the tunnel, floating past the spider, tickling Tobin's whiskers. Raising his head, Tobin sniffed, closing his eyes, breathing in slow and steady. His stomach rolled as he let the spider's odor fill his senses.

"What are you doing?" Wiley set a paw on his shoulder, but Tobin waved him off.

Decay, like rotting plants. Oil . . . a burned scent. Acidic. An underlying scent of . . . milk. Dandelion.

Tobin's eyes shot wide open. "Oh no."

Just then the spider froze, bobbing its body up and

down, swirling a leg in the air. Finding the breeze, looking for a way out.

The spider again lurched forward and Tobin took a small step after it, but Wiley thumped a paw on his tail. Tobin turned to see Wiley nodding back toward Talia. His sister's eyes were wide and her fur was spiked. She put her paw against the tunnel wall.

"Another spider's coming," she hissed.

Tobin set his ear beside her paw.

Click, click, click, click—scrape.

A second spider, following the same trail as this one. How much time before it rounded the corner? Tobin looked back at the bundle inching farther away.

Squeak.

"Did you hear that?" said Tobin. The call was faint, but unmistakable. Almost like a baby bird peep, but more breathy. More familiar.

A paw clamped on Tobin's shoulder. Talia leaned into him, her voice trembling. "Is that *our* new baby?"

Tobin's mind began spinning: *Mom. Dad. The baby . . .* until a sudden pain in his tail quickly cleared his head. He turned to see it drop from Wiley's jaws.

"Talia said"—Wiley's eyes narrowed as he tried to hold his attention—"there's another spider coming. I heard the squeak, too, but we need to hide. Do you hear me?"

"It's just . . ." Tobin trailed off as he looked back to the baby-snatching spider.

It reached the source of the breeze—a small lookout hole in the tunnel wall. The spider jabbed at the opening, ripping chunks of the wall down around it. The frenzy of its digging jostled the websack, and two tiny legs poked through the webbing, along with a little gray tail.

"No," Tobin whispered.

Another pinch on Tobin's tail.

"I'll bite your tail clean off if you don't hide now!" said Wiley.

And there was Talia beside him. Tobin nodded. "We know which way it's heading. Let's climb outside."

Wiley ducked into a nearby passage, a steep, narrow tunnel. They skittered upward. The passageway forked, one path lit by shards of daylight and filled with fresh air. This trail led outside.

Tobin sniffed as he neared the exit. The rain had stopped. A small ridge with just enough space for three sets of paws jutted from the mouth of the opening.

"There." Talia pointed down.

The spider's powerful legs were breaking through the crumbling wall. The arachnid stepped out, and only then did its enormity become clear. The spider stood and stretched. Its size rivaled that of a full-grown toad.

Despite its bulkiness, the spider nimbly scuttled down the slant of the burrow wall to the forest floor. Tobin waited for it to run away. But it just stood there.

Instead, a much smaller spider, but with the same coloring, stepped out from the bushes. It scurried to the big hunter, stood directly in front of its patch of quivering red eyes, and began bobbing up and down.

Wiley spoke. "What's it doing?"

"I have no idea," Tobin replied, entranced by the macabre display unfolding.

The giant spider then raised one front leg, swirled it in the air, then set it back down. After this cue, the smaller spider climbed right up the big leg and across the spider's back, and began inspecting the websack.

A dizzying wave of terror washed over Tobin. Was he about to witness the unthinkable? After all the worry about his new pinkling sibling being born healthy, to think he would lose it to this monster this way was unbearable. Despite the tremble in his legs, Tobin tried taking a step forward, but Wiley again clamped down on his tail.

"M-mice have many enemies." Tobin forced the quiver from his voice. "But I never knew spiders were on that list."

"This can't be happening," whispered Wiley.

Talia stepped forward. "No. Look, the little spider's fixing the websack."

"What?" Tobin blinked hard, refocusing on the scene and hoping to see what Talia saw. Sure enough, the smaller spider quickly but precisely added a new, glossy layer of webbing around the pinkling. "But why?" Tobin asked.

Inspection and repairs complete, the smaller spider hopped off its big counterpart's back. The beastly one turned to face the burrow once again. It stomped its two front legs; left, right—*stomp-stomp, stomp-stomp.*

"Communicating," Tobin guessed. "Calling to the other spider?" A moment later, another set of legs sprouted from the fresh hole. Tobin checked its rear digits and drew a ragged breath in relief. "Look, this one didn't catch anything."

The new spider hurried to its counterpart, probing its face and body with a spindly leg. The first spider turned, raising its catch for inspection.

"I can't watch anymore." Talia buried her face in Tobin's side.

Tobin couldn't speak; his throat felt as dry as sunbaked mud. The newcomer's pointy leg stretched forth and gently nudged the webbed bundle. The pinkling squeaked. The newcomer swirled its front leg, and once again the small spider appeared and climbed aboard, but finding no sack to repair, it simply hopped off and scurried toward the bushes. The big hunters turned to follow its lead.

A sudden numbness overwhelmed Tobin. *Our pinkling. We're going to lose another pinkling. Unless . . .*

Talia looked around. "Where is everyone else?"

Her question snapped Tobin from his daze. "Yeah, shouldn't the Eldermice be following them out? Where—" Tobin stopped. There was a Rule:

Rule #15: If the burrow is damaged, bind it fast or the colony will not last.

Tobin's heart sank. "They're patching the burrow, fixing however those things got in." How had they gotten in? Had the storm damaged the burrow so badly? How had they made it into his family's quarters? And how'd the spider get the pinkling away from—

Tobin's blood pumped. A growl grew in his chest. The dizzy feeling was back.

Wiley's paw clamped his shoulder. "Don't even think about it."

"I have to do something!" Tobin looked down. The spiders started scuttling back toward the woods, near the creek. Tobin took a step forward but stopped.

Rule #8: Never pursue a predator. Never.

But his mom would lose another baby if he didn't do

something. If she was still alive. *No. Of course she is. Those spiders couldn't take down a group of full-grown mice.*

"I have to follow the spiders, okay?" Tobin looked to Talia. "I saw it. I saw our baby's gray tail. I smelled the milk and mom's dandelion scent. I can't just let them go. Tell Mom and Dad that I followed it, and if there's a way, I'll bring our pinkling home. Mom's not going to lose another baby."

Her face twisted with fright. "What? No, Tobin, you can't. Rule Eight, remember?"

Tobin's paws rocked back and forth on the ledge. "I know what it says. Please, Wiley, will you take her home?"

Wiley's chest puffed. "Not without you."

"Please," Tobin pleaded. "If they put the websack down, even for a second, I could grab it. I could outrun them!"

"Not by yourself," Talia said softly.

Wiley looked at the spiders then back to Tobin. "I'm going with you."

"But I need you to take Talia—" Tobin began, but never finished.

Talia leaped off the ledge, ending the argument for everyone.

five

THERE WAS NOTHING TOBIN could do but watch the wind rush through Talia's fur as she fell. *At least the ground is damp!* Tobin thought with a wince as she landed.

Wiley clucked his tongue. "Hey, she landed in the crabgrass. That's a nice jump."

Tobin gazed downward and watched Talia shake her head before she looked up. "What're you guys waiting for?" she called.

"Right." Tobin nodded, rubbing a waterdrop off his brow. "I guess she showed us the way." Tobin squatted low, ready to jump. "No turning back. You coming?"

"I've always wanted to try this," Wiley said, peering over the ledge. "Never thought Talia would beat me to it."

Tobin whipped his tail and centered his balance. "Aim

to the left of her," he said, then he leaped.

Air swooshed through his fur. The sensation didn't last long. Tall tips of crabgrass brushed his paws and he hit the ground. The spongy roots helped absorb his fall, but it still hurt when his chin slammed the ground.

"Are you okay?"

Between the shimmering green blades he saw Talia's pink nose, followed by her eyes, bulged with worry.

"Tobin? Are you okay?" she repeated.

"Uh-huh." He blinked and shook his head. "I'm fine."

"Are you mad?" she asked.

He felt like yelling—but that's never a good idea outside the burrow. A harsh whisper would have to do. "You need to be way, *wa-a-ay* more careful. I can't handle two Wileys."

"But I knew you wouldn't let me—"

A nearby patch of crabgrass shook, and Talia pointed. "Speaking of Wiley, he's a little off target."

Tobin turned his head, filling his lungs with air until his chest swelled. *"Tchirr, tchirr,"* he called out.

A moment passed.

"Tchirr, tchirr," Wiley called back, then wove through the grass beside them. "Ah, there you are. So, we're all in this together, right?"

Like there's a choice? Tobin nodded. "Looks like the spiders are heading toward the fallen tree. If we take cover in those boxwood shrubs, we might be able to work our way down—"

Wiley groaned.

Tobin bit his lip. Of course. Rule-bending Wiley probably wants to charge right after the spiders, taking no cover at all, forgetting that we have a mouseling in tow.

Tobin held out a paw. "Before you say a word, Wiley, remember, Talia is with us, so we need to do things by the Rules."

Wiley nodded, his paw tapping. "Yeah, uh-huh. But the boxwood shrubs? No. Those bushes are so thick a slug could barely squirm through. The spiders will be long gone."

Sludge. Tobin scratched his ear. Wiley had a point. But they couldn't exactly traipse after the spiders in the wide open, either.

Rule #4: Instinct and logic combined plot the successful course.

Was there a compromise?

"How about we don't tunnel through the shrubs," said Tobin. "We'll just run beneath their fringes for cover until we reached the creek, then cut back to the fallen tree. There's plenty of cover at the creek bed. We'll scout the spiders from there."

Wiley cocked an ear. "That'll work."

Tobin looked to Talia, and she gave a quick nod.

"I'll volunteer to lead as Pathleader," Tobin began, "then you in the middle, Tal. And Wiley, you stay close behind her."

"Got it," Wiley answered, with surprisingly no trace of levity in his voice. He was already peeking through the crabgrass, sniffing intently.

Tobin poked his own nose through the thick blades. Only a few hare-leaps down a pebbly ridge to the shrubs. He focused on his endpoint then scanned the sky and surroundings. *Clear.* Tobin focused again on the endpoint, and *GO.*

He burst from the clump of grass; two swishing sounds behind him meant Talia and Wiley were on his tail. He sailed down the rain-slicked slope. Half sliding, half tumbling, he landed under the boughs of the boxwood shrub with a *THUD.*

Tobin dived to the right, just before Talia and Wiley slammed in after him.

The three looked each other, nodding in satisfaction. The unruly shrub, no taller than a fawn, had plenty of low-hanging branches that provided cover from above. Not *total* cover, but it would do. Tobin sniffed and pushed his nose through the piles of wind-strewn forest litter, perfect for ground cover.

Proper scouting procedure—as explained in the Rules of Rodentia: Articles of Exploration—requires that if mice are to travel in a group, one mouse must act as Pathleader, with their job being to analyze the surroundings to deduce the safest way forward.

Tobin scratched the fur behind his ear. Had any Pathleaders been in the pursuit of predators before? A footstep, just outside the shrubs, snapped Tobin from his thoughts. *Click-clack*—the telltale sound of claws hitting ground. Bird claws. Then the sound of powerful lungs drawing breath.

Kraak-kraak-kraak-kraak!

A great heron. The ground litter trembled beneath Tobin's paws from the bleating call. Tobin stood frozen. A clawed foot entered his line of vision. Talons curving down from orange, leathery skin, attached to a leg as thick as a sunflower stalk. The heron called again. This time, some distance away, another heron shrieked back. Excited gurgles bubbled from the huge bird's chest. It took a few shaky steps, nearly stepping on a bullfrog.

Tobin squinted, bracing himself for the gruesome spearing he knew was coming. But the heron launched into the air, leaving its potential prey to hop into the bushes.

"I've never seen a heron pass up a meal," Wiley muttered.

Tobin nodded. "The creatures of the wood are still shaken from the storm. Even the hunters are off their game. We need to take advantage of it."

Reaching the canopy of the crashed tree, Tobin stepped out from under the shrub. The tree had sliced the creek bed, pools of mud swirling beneath it. He nodded to some soggy squirrels still pulling themselves from the muck.

"Poor things," whispered Talia.

Wiley shook his head. "Them? Those squirrels are lucky to be alive. See those vultures circling up there? Once the dust settles, they'll pick through this tree and find the critters that didn't survive."

Talia shuddered. "That's really awful, Wiley."

Wiley shrugged. "Maybe. But it's better than having dead animals lying around, stinking up everything."

"You really have a way with words," Tobin said, and shook his head. A shimmer of black near the creek caught his eye. He rose onto his hind legs, peering between fluttering leaves and broken branches.

"The spiders." Tobin blinked twice before looking again, hoping what he thought he saw wasn't really happening.

His heart sank to his paws. "They're using the fallen tree like a bridge to cross the creek. They are escaping with our pinkling."

"No," Talia gasped, raising herself up to see the spectacle.

Wiley's forehead scrunched with concern as he stared at Tobin. "What are we going to do?"

Follow them.

The very thought made Tobin's head swim. "I need a better look." Tobin drew in a steadying breath and leaped into the mangled branches, scurrying along the twisted, broken limbs until he neared the tree trunk. He stopped short of stepping out onto the exposed, bare bark of the tree trunk.

The trunk itself was as thick around as a small boulder, so there was plenty of dry surface to cross—the creek water only splashed over the sides a bit. And really, if the spiders could manage it . . .

"I'm going over." The words tumbled from Tobin's mouth before he could think any further. He looked back to Talia and Wiley.

Talia rubbed her paws together, glancing from the tree bridge back to Tobin. "Maybe we should go back and get Dad, tell him where the spiders went."

"There's no time for all of us to go back." Tobin looked back to the spiders, focusing on the one with their pinkling in tow. The arachnids were already across, already climbing down the big knot of tree roots ripped up from the ground. "You don't have to come, either of you." Tobin narrowed his eyes as he spoke.

"You're not going alone," Talia said, and she stopped rubbing her paws together. "I don't think I've ever heard of any burrow mice crossing the creek before."

No specific Rule about creek-crossing came to mind, but Tobin remembered again—

Rule #8: Never pursue a predator. Never.

Tobin coughed and cleared his throat. "I think our pinkling might be the first to cross it."

"Then we'll be the first to cross voluntarily," said Wiley.

"Look," Tobin began, then blinked for a moment, trying to will the words to come. "I don't expect, or even want, you two to come with me. This is beyond dangerous, this is . . ."

"Reckless?" Wiley offered.

Tobin cocked his head. "Beyond reckless."

"No." Talia slapped a paw to the ground, a subtle growl in her voice. "Charging the spiders directly would've been reckless. Running through the woods without a plan or path would be reckless. What we're doing—together—is special, Tobin. And it's working. We can keep up with the spiders. We just need our chance to grab our pinkling and run."

Tobin looked at the fallen tree before them, then back to the faces of two of the most important mice in his life. They weren't budging. Tobin nodded. "Okay. But Talia is right. We talk, we agree on a plan, and we follow it."

Wiley and Talia both nodded.

"All right." Tobin turned back to the tree bridge. "Let's stay close together. Me, then Talia, then you, Wiley." Tobin looked to Talia. "Grab my tail if you need to."

Talia lowered her head and grabbed the tip of his tail in her mouth. "Is dis gud nuf?"

"Perfect," Tobin said. He turned to face the creek. Suddenly, his paws felt as heavy as clams. He knew these woods, but across the creek? That was unknown territory. He couldn't move.

"Tobin?" Wiley called from behind.

"One sec." Tobin drew in a deep breath and shut his

eyes. What if they didn't go? *Sure, Mom. I could have saved the baby, but I really didn't want to cross a log.*

No way.

Tobin opened his eyes. He scanned the sky. All clear. He focused on the creek bank ahead and called over his shoulder. "Okay, quick and steady. Here we go."

He took a step, then another. Step, step, step, until they were over the creek. The bark was wet and soft. His claws dug in easily. Step, step—tug. Glancing back, he saw Talia's eyes fixed on the rushing water.

"Tal, I need to lead you across, not drag you." Tobin forced himself to smile. Talia nodded, so he moved ahead. Splashes of water soaked his feet and belly. At the center of the tree bridge the current was faster, sending splays of water that doused their whiskers. Again, Talia froze, squeaking a muffled yelp.

Tobin had to holler. "If the spiders made it across, we can make it across, right?"

Talia replied with a squeal-like grunt.

Taking that for a yes, Tobin continued. Water splashed inside his ears. He snorted water from his nose. All he could smell was algae and wet bark, but they were almost across. The creek water was overwhelming—and a Rule blazed to memory:

Rule #2: Never become blinded by a singular worry; there are plenty of ways to die.

The Rule only managed to trip his panic trigger. There was more danger than the river below. *We're exposed, look up!*

Hawk.

six

THE HAWK WAS ALREADY beginning its dive, its beak open and talons unfurling from beneath its feathered body.

Move or die. Tobin thought furiously, realizing there was only one way to go.

He spun around, shoving Talia into the creek.

His eyes met Wiley's, and his friend leaped.

Tobin sprang off the tree bridge with every ounce of force he could muster, just as talons sliced the air above him; the scent of death brushed his nose. The hawk's angry screech cut out as Tobin plunged into the creek.

His limbs tingled with the shock of cold water. The current tumbled him downstream like a leaf in the wind. Air—he needed air! Tobin snapped his muscles, legs pumping, pushing up through the murky green water into the light above. His chest burned until his muzzle broke the surface. He gasped in a lungful of air as he paddled toward shore.

Over the ripples of waves, a line of cattails sprouted from the water's edge. Tobin kicked toward them, swishing his tail, his legs searing with exhaustion. A piece of driftwood poked out invitingly from between the reeds. He stretched his neck, clamping down on the wood with his teeth. Grabbing the plank of wood with his paws, he heaved himself up, muscles shaking.

For a few moments he lay still. His cold, waterlogged body soaked in warmth from the sunbaked slab. "Tal?" he croaked. He coughed and tried again. "Talia! Wiley?"

"Shh! Tobin, be quiet!"

Wiley!

Tobin craned his neck, looking into the towering cattails. "Where are you?"

"Look to your right. Slowly! Do not rock that driftwood."

Tobin turned his head. A soaking-wet Wiley clung to the brown tuft of a cattail reed. And below, an equally drenched Talia pulled herself up into the crook of a sprouting cattail leaf.

"Listen, Tobin," said Wiley, his paw outstretched. "Do *not* panic, but—there's a monster catfish checking you out."

That's when Tobin felt it. A nudge against the drift-wood—not the rocking of the waves, but a bump. Every few seconds—bump! He understood, and his stomach turned. "Is this fish trying to knock me into the water so it can *eat* me?"

Wiley grimaced. "Yeah, I think so. You're gonna have to jump, but wait till I say go. I've seen catfish snap drag-onflies right from the air."

"Sludge." Tobin dug his claws in deep as another slam rocked him harder.

Fish bait. He'd gone from hawk food to fish bait.

"Get low," Wiley urged, a tinge of panic wavered in his voice. "It's poking its head up."

Impossible! Yet a fishy odor crossed Tobin's nose. It couldn't be . . .

Tobin slowly turned his head. The fur on his nose stood straight up as he stared directly into the unblink-ing, beady eye of a catfish. Its unfeeling gaze fell over him like a cold blanket; its mottled, brown head bobbed above the surface like a rotten melon. Tobin gagged as the reek of fish breath filled his nose. The catfish swayed its head away from the driftwood, then with a splash and lurch of its body, it thwacked its head against the board.

Tobin dug his claws deeper into the damp wood and snapped his gaze to Wiley. "It's trying to knock me off!"

Wiley yelled back, but the catfish thrashed again, and the splashing water swallowed up Wiley's words.

The fish slapped at the slab again, this time with its tail, then it lifted its head. Loosened lumps of fish slime rolled from its forehead, dropping into its gaping mouth. Tobin turned his head, gagging and gasping for a breath that didn't reek of fish.

For a moment, all was still.

Tobin sucked in a quick breath, looked back, but the fish was gone. He looked up to Wiley, desperate for directions, what to do next.

Wiley shouted, "Jump now! It's under you—you're gonna get flipped!"

Tobin yanked his claws from the wood and darted to the edge of the slab. Just as he readied to jump, the catfish pummeled the board from beneath. Tobin's body flattened as the wood sailed upward. Tobin saw a cattail tuft from the corner of his eye. He sprang, grabbing the caterpillar-shaped poof. Spongy seeds came loose between his claws, fluttering through his grasp, so he chomped at the inner stalk. His jaws clenched the tall reed and he circled his hind legs around the stem. He clung to the reed, hanging upside down over the fish. The catfish snapped its mouth over and over, its soggy whiskers flopping. Just for good measure, Tobin wrapped his dangling tail around the stalk. But the reed held, and the catfish couldn't jump high enough to get him.

The catfish mouthed silent but angry protests below.

"Give it up," Tobin shouted. "I am not coming back down!" The fish thrashed in the shallows a few more times, then flopped its way back into the deeper water of the creek.

"Tobin, over here."

Despite hanging upside down, Tobin managed to turn his head to see Wiley perched on a cattail just a few reeds over.

"Let's get to shore," Wiley said.

"Yeah," Tobin croaked. He looked at Talia. She sat curled in a ball, one leaf blade below Wiley. Or was she above Wiley? Hard to tell when he was upside down.

Wiley climbed onto Talia's leaf. "C'mon, Tal, everything's okay."

Talia didn't budge, so Wiley nudged her with his nose. "Let's move, cotton ball." She finally peeked up, big eyes peering over her tail.

"Hey, up here." Tobin waved. "We're all fine. Follow Wiley."

She uncurled and glared at the water, eventually sliding down the stalk. Tobin turned himself around and shimmied down his own cattail, leaping off toward the shore. He landed in a mushy pile of decaying plants.

"We're heading your way," Wiley called.

Good. Tobin's leg muscles were tired and his chin throbbed. He felt like a pine cone that hit every branch on the way down.

"Hey." Wiley scurried over. "That was some serious claw work. I don't know how you—wow." Wiley clamped a paw over his nose. "Do you know you smell like dead fish?"

"You think?" Tobin answered. "You guys might want to back up." He shimmied, but clumps of creek mud still stuck to his fur.

Talia cringed. "I think you need a puddle."

"Sludge." Tobin snatched his tail in his paws, yanking off stuck bits of dead grass. "Hopefully we can find one on the way. We need to get back to the spider trail."

"Don't you want to rest a minute?" Wiley asked.

"Well . . ." Tobin tugged at a sludgy clump of mud behind his ear. "Ugh. Maybe I could use a minute. Would you mind taking a quick look ahead?"

"No problem," Wiley said, before looking Tobin up and down. "Hopefully I'll see a puddle."

"Hopefully." Tobin winced as he pulled the sludge clump from behind his ear, probably taking some fur with it. "How did you and Wiley get to shore so fast?"

"I think we hopped into the right current." Talia stretched and flexed her front legs. "And thank goodness for paddling lessons."

"Hey, come look at this," Wiley called, pointing his paw toward a patch of quivering swamp fronds. Out scuttled a mottled blue crayfish. About half their size and looking for bits of dead fish or bugs to eats, it twitched its antennae, shuffling its legs and moving onto the narrow strip of beach. It wasn't a threat to them. But it was worth paying attention to.

Rule #6: If you find yourself in a strange place, take your cues from the locals.

Tobin watched the crayfish. It scuttled from the cover of the fronds, zigzagging across the beach. It picked up tiny particles with its pincers, inspecting each one, hoping for something edible.

Most important, it seemed at ease.

"If that crayfish feels safe enough to move around, maybe we are, too," Tobin said.

Talia added, "Nothing's jumping out of the rocks to catch it."

Wiley whipped his tail. "I'd sure like to get my tail end back in the woods."

69

"Me too." Tobin craned his neck, looking at the climb in front of them. "We just need to get up these rocks. Ready?"

"First"—Wiley held up a paw—"we need to make one stop."

Tobin followed Wiley's gaze to a small indent in a rock on the creek bed. A puddle.

"Please?" said Wiley.

"My pleasure," Tobin agreed. He deftly skimmed one rock over, then rolled in the shallow pool, scraping his coat against the coarse rock. After three quick rolls, he shimmied and jumped back. "Better?"

"Much," Wiley answered.

"Then let's go." Tobin stretched his hind legs and did a quick skyward scan. Seeing nothing, he bolted. The crayfish's claws jerked high in surprise when he streaked past. Tobin scrambled atop a boulder, hopped up to the next, and finally darted behind a broken pine branch stuck between two rocks.

He waited just a breath for Talia and Wiley to fall in line behind him. Right as they did, Tobin readied himself to jump again. A shrill *chip!* caught his attention, and he froze.

He saw Talia and Wiley freeze beneath the branch,

as well. Talia tilted her head, her left ear pivoting as she listened. She whispered, her voice as soft as paw pads on grass, "I know that sound."

It came again, echoing down the rocks.

Chip-chip-trill. Chip-chip-trill.

As the call finished, Tobin looked to Talia.

"It's a chipmunk," she said. "We're in its territory, but I don't think it's aggressive."

Tobin raised an eyebrow. "You don't think? Can you be sure?"

She looked up as she considered. "No, but remember Rodent Studies class? I'm pretty sure there'd be foot-thumping if it was mad."

Wiley shrugged. "I think she's right. Let's have a look. After all, we can't stay here out in the open."

"True," said Tobin, and the three peeked out from beneath the pine-needle-covered branch.

Perched above them was a chipmunk; a very sleek, especially long-bodied chipmunk. Its dark eyes bore into Tobin. Did that stare mean curiosity—or aggression?

"Hello," called Talia.

Tobin nearly jumped out his hide. "Tal!"

"What?" She raised a paw, gesturing to the striped rodent. "It obviously wants to talk."

"How do you—" Tobin started but then stopped. The chipmunk dipped its head, then beat its tail wildly against the rock. Rays of late-day sun caught its chestnut fur, contrasted starkly by the black-and-white streaks running down its back. The chipmunk seemed leaner, maybe even tougher, than the few he'd met on their side of the creek.

It jerked its head back and chirped, beckoning them forward.

Tobin took a deep breath. "Okay. You're right. It's calling us up."

"Told you." A smile crept onto Talia's face and delight filled her eyes. "We're meeting a chipmunk!"

seven

"I'VE NEVER BEEN IN a chipmunk den." Talia rubbed her paws together with anticipation as she crept forward. "Do you think it saw the spiders?"

"Maybe. But, stop a second. Let's be careful. That chipmunk is three times our size." Tobin's many thoughts swirled through his mind like tadpoles trapped in a puddle. Too much was happening. Never mind the spiders and the agitated chipmunk; he was also seeing a whole new side of his sister. "You really think it's okay to follow this chipmunk, Tal?"

"Of course," she answered, then tapped a hind paw, apparently eager to move on. "We learned about them in our Rodent Studies class last season. Its ears were tilted forward, not pressed back to its head. So all the tail beating and head jerking was to attract us." She then rose on her hind legs and sniffed the air. "Do you smell that? You can just make out the chipmunk's scent. It's a male. So if he were unhappy with us, we'd have been charged by now."

"Wow." Tobin nodded his appreciation. "Guess I don't need to ask if you passed Rodent Studies."

"I did pretty good, I guess," Talia answered.

"Pretty good?" Wiley chuckled. "My little brother Smudge's in your brood group. He said being partners with you in RS class is great. It's like being paired with a teacher who's also fun."

Talia dipped her head, the tips of her ears turning a shade of pink. "Oh, I don't know about that."

Wiley looked up the hill. "Well, either way, you're right on this. That chipmunk could've dropped a surprise attack on us if he wanted a fight."

"True," said Tobin. "And we are heading in his direction anyway. Might as well stop by."

Tobin pulled himself up one boulder, then another, only taking his eyes off the perched chipmunk to look for footholds. The striped stranger watched, too, poised perfectly still. Tobin lost sight of the chipmunk when he scaled the very rock it was perched on, and when he crested the top, the chipmunk was gone.

Wiley climbed up beside him. "What? Where did that toad-turd of a rodent run off to?"

"Look," said Talia, "in that crevice."

Tobin stared at a cragged space between rocks. Squinting, he could just make out onyx eyes staring back.

The chipmunk finally spoke. "You're not from this side of the creek. Why did you cross to our side?"

For a moment Tobin was intrigued to hear rodent-tongue from the chipmunk. The nuances between species always amazed him. Like chipmunks having surprisingly low voices.

Tobin decided to just be honest. "We crossed for a good reason. We're following something."

The chipmunk nodded slowly. "Perhaps spiders? Carrying a webbed bundle?"

"You saw them?" Talia stepped forward.

"I did," the chipmunk answered. "You've never had Arakni on your side of the creek, have you?"

Tobin cocked an ear. "Have what?"

"A-rak-ni," The rodent annunciated, his tail flicked with each syllable.

"Never heard of 'em," Wiley said.

The chipmunk wriggled his nose. "I thought not. My name is Camrik. Please, come in. I should tell you about these spiders you're tracking and know nothing about."

Tobin drew a sharp breath, not sure what to say.

"Look at it this way, young mouse," said Camrik, his eyes narrowing when Tobin hesitated to follow him. "Not knowing a flea's flick about the spiders you're chasing is far, *far* more dangerous than a short conversation with me."

Well, that was probably true. "All right," Tobin said, and the onyx eyes disappeared into the crevice.

"C'mon," Wiley urged. "We've been in the open too long anyway; it's probably best we keep moving."

"Yeah," Tobin agreed, stepping inside the entryway. A long tunnel, just tall enough for a chipmunk, ran deep into the earth of the hillside. They walked until the passageway opened into a chamber. There, Camrik waited for them in the center of a sparse den. A pile of cattail fluff rested against one wall for sleeping, and a mound of seeds lay stacked opposite to that. That was it.

"Hope you find my dwelling comfortable enough," Camrik said.

Talia gazed across the domed ceiling. "It's a lot different than a mouse burrow."

The rocky soil gave the den a clammy feel. And there was only one tunnel in and out. Mice preferred tunnels— lots and lots of tunnels.

Their host smiled, looking amused. "I imagine it is different. We chipmunks are more of a solitary bunch."

"Camrik," Tobin started, anxious for answers, "my name's Tobin. This is my sister, Talia, and our friend Wiley."

Camrik nodded. "It's a pleasure to meet you spider-chasing mice. I had no idea mice were so daring."

"We're usually not," Tobin said flatly.

Wiley shot Tobin a glance. "Speak for yourself."

"Anyway," Tobin continued, "you were going to tell us about the spiders."

Camrik's brow furrowed. "Yes. I'm a bit of an expert. As I said, we call them Arakni, on this side of the creek. I'm afraid that fallen tree has given them passage to your side."

Talia cocked her head. "What does the tree have to do with anything?"

"This storm." Camrik looked upward as though he could still see the sky even in his cave. "It knocked over that tree, and it must have landed right beside your burrow. There were hunter spiders in that treetop. When it crashed by your home, the spiders simply went back to work. Gathering prey."

"I've never seen a spider even half their size before," Wiley said.

"The Arakni come in many sizes, but they're more like monsters than spiders." Camrik's ears flattened to his head, betraying a fierceness that raised the fur on Tobin's neck. Camrik shook his head when he saw Tobin's fright. "Forgive me. It's been a while since I've had any visitors."

"It's all right." Tobin spoke fast, trying to keep the jitters from creeping into his voice. "Please continue."

Camrik took a deep breath, seeming to steady his nerves. He continued. "My mother told us that long ago, generations before she was even born, Arakni were rare. Almost a legend, except that every now and then, someone would stumble upon the shell-like remains of a dead Arakni. Elders would warn young pups, 'Don't roam too far, or the Arakni will get you.'"

Talia shivered. "That's awful."

Camrik nodded. "Something changed years ago, when my mother was only a pup. The Arakni grew in numbers. The small, quick-moving scouts and the larger, dreaded hunters would comb the forest looking for prey."

"So that's what we saw?" asked Tobin.

"Yes," Talia agreed. "And we saw their horrible bouncing and stomping as they talked to each other."

"Yes." Camrik nodded. "You see how they have evolved. What was once only dozens grew into hundreds of spiders. Now, each spring they come out, hunting together in a giant swarm."

Wiley's ears flattened. "That's plain horrific."

"They come out once a year?" Tobin asked, shivering at the thought of such a hunting party.

"Yes." Camrik looked up, as if a vision of the night sky replaced his dirt ceiling. "For one cycle of the moon, the Arakni plunder our woods. They capture prey and then scuttle it back to whatever infernal chasm they crawled out of."

Wiley looked at Tobin. "It's a swarm of spiders. A *swarm*."

"Yes." Camrik raised an eyebrow. "Tell me, how much do the three of you know about bees?"

The three mice looked at each other.

"Um," Tobin started, "I guess we know not to bother them or they'll sting?"

"True," Camrik said. "But they're so much more complex than that. In a colony, different bees have different jobs. There are gatherers, builders, a queen. Working together, the hive will succeed. Ants, by the way, also have a similar structure."

"Okay," Tobin said, "what does this have to do with the spiders?"

Camrik took a deep breath. "Ants and bees are successful, resourceful, and typically don't bother us because they're not hunting us. But the Arakni . . ." Camrik shook his head. "As near as I can tell, they are the only spiders who've adopted this structure, to live as a society. And it's been successful. Too successful."

Tobin gleaned at least one silver lining in Camrik's dismal load of information. "They're gathering victims to eat *later*," said Tobin. "We need to find where they're stashing all these websacks, and that's where we'll find our pinkling."

"I respect your bravery, each of you." The chipmunk began to pace along the wall between the bedding and seed pile. Tobin noticed the groove in the floor. Obviously Camrik paced a lot. "My paws have been in your path. I've lost—we've all, on this side of the creek, lost someone to the Arakni."

Talia shuddered. "I can't imagine having to see those monsters every spring."

Camrik stopped. His ears drooped and he spoke softly. "Unless something's done about the tree bridge, the Arakni will be an even bigger problem for your burrow next spring."

The pink drained from Talia's nose. "Oh no. They could come back!"

"And next time, they'll bring more Arakni with them," Camrik finished.

Could the Eldermice hold off an *entire pack* of Arakni? The burrow was in more danger than anyone back home even knew. Tobin should run home, tell the Eldermice all he'd learned, gather more mice to help rescue the pinkling—except, time. Time was something a newborn pinkling doesn't have a lot of.

"We'll worry about stopping an Arakni invasion later," Tobin said. "First we need to find our pinkling."

Camrik nodded. "There are three things you should know before embarking on the Arakni trail. First, the hunt is over tonight. Any Arakni you follow will lead you back to the lair."

"Got it," said Tobin.

"Wait." Wiley raised a paw. "That means they won't go back to the Great Burrow this hunting cycle?"

"Correct." Camrik continued, "Secondly, their lair is more than a day's journey from here. My mother tried to follow them once as well. But the Arakni traveled too far; she didn't want to leave us pups . . ." Camrik swallowed and cleared his throat. "Us pups that were left."

Tobin shook his head. How could life be so different just a deer's-leap across the creek?

"I'm sorry, Camrik," said Talia.

"Don't worry yourself, little mouseling." Camrik forced a smile. "You needn't fret about me. You've got bigger concerns."

"You said there were three things we need to know?" Tobin asked.

"Yes," said Camrik. "Lastly, an Arakni carrying a websack is practically in a trance. All it thinks about is getting home. They're relatively easy to follow."

"Sounds simple enough," Wiley said.

Camrik's eyes narrowed. "But the Arakni returning without a websack is near mad with rage. Those are the ones you need to watch out for."

Tobin shivered. He was raised to know the forest was always watching him, he'd just never imagined its eyes were red.

eight

"THAT'S JUST NASTY." WILEY shook his head as he sniffed the air.

Tobin saw a hint of a smile tug the corners of Camrik's mouth. "It's a foul stench, yes. But it does make the Arakni easier to follow."

"Thanks for getting us back on track, Camrik," said Tobin. The four rodents sat at the forest's edge nestled beneath a giant fallen maple leaf. Camrik had shown them the best way to track the Arakni—unfortunately it was by their terrible smell.

"It's no bother," Camrik answered, suddenly pressing himself low to the ground. "But you may not need to follow the stench. Look ahead."

Tobin flattened, his eyes following Camrik's gaze.

"You could just follow that," Camrik finished.

An Arakni scuttled over the ridge of rocks they'd just climbed. Only a hare-leap away, it crept past them, a bundle clasped between its back pinchers. Tobin raised his chin to get a better look. The creature in the sack wriggled more than the pinkling, its legs springing against the stretchy webbing.

Wiley leaned in beside him. "A cricket?"

Tobin nodded, thinking back to the cricket he'd eaten a week ago. "Never thought I'd feel bad for a bug."

"As long as that Arakni already has a catch," said Camrik, "you can safely follow it."

Talia's ears perked. "That's better than smelling our way there."

"Then you have to go, quickly," Camrik said. His striped forehead creased with worry. "Stop by my den on your way home. Once I know you've made it back to your burrow, I'd like to destroy that tree bridge."

"But how?" asked Tobin.

Talia swished her tail. "Hey, that Arakni is getting away. C'mon!"

"You'll see when you get back. Just hurry." Camrik raised his paw and recited an ancient Rodentia farewell: "Swiftly and safely, be on your way."

Tobin, Talia, and Wiley each raised a paw in return. "Swiftly and safely, till another day."

Camrik nodded. He dashed from beneath the leaf, disappearing quickly in the forest brush.

Tobin turned his attention back to the cricket-carrying Arakni. It scuttled over a pile of pine needles and headed deeper into the woods. How many times had Tobin looked upon this stretch of forest from back home, across the creek? But now, standing on its edge, a shiver ran down his spine. Trees, so tall he couldn't see their peaks, swayed and creaked in the breeze. Tiny flecks of sunlight poked through the needle-covered limbs, speckling the messy forest floor. The ancient woods provided lots of cover. But what else lurked in the litter?

"Stay close," Tobin whispered. Neither Talia nor Wiley took their eyes from the woods. They nodded in silence.

Tobin lowered his head. His ears pricked forward as he peered through the brush ahead. Minus the giant spider they were tracking, it seemed safe enough to move. He darted into the woods, first diving beneath a fallen tree branch. His paw pads felt the vibration of Talia, then Wiley, slide in behind him.

Feeling safe, he hopped atop the branch. There, two hare-leaps ahead, he spotted the Arakni navigating through the biggest toadstool patch Tobin had ever seen. The oversize spider was attempting to wobble its way over the orange-and-white-spotted mushroom caps. Tobin knew that unlike the giant spider, they'd have no trouble slinking between the toadstool stalks. Raising his nose, Tobin sniffed the air, and his stomach growled. The carrot-colored fungi could take care of two problems— hide them from the spider and provide a little snack.

Tobin darted, plunging between two spongy stems. Wriggling into the thick of the toadstools, the smell of mushroom meat stirred a fierce hunger.

Rule #21: Like a leaping squirrel missing its branch, a missed opportunity cannot be saved.

Tobin looked over his shoulder. "Let's grab a bite. Who knows when we'll have another chance."

Wiley needed no further convincing, chomping into the nearest stem. Talia sidled up alongside Tobin, plucking a smaller fungus from the ground to nibble on. Tobin stretched up and swiped his paws through the fleshy, gill-like filling of the toadstool cap above him, shoving the moist morsels into his mouth. As he chewed, he eyed the shadow of the Arakni scuttling above.

Tobin swallowed the last bits of mushroom mash. "We can eat more along the way. Let's keep moving."

Onward they wove through the toadstools, until the patch gave way to large clumps of ferns. Vines of forest grapes laced along the ground. All the while, the Arakni seemed oblivious to their presence, trudging ahead with purpose, never breaking its path, preferring to climb over a stone than walk around it.

From beneath a thicket of vines, Tobin studied the trees, noting the disks of fungus that clung to the tree trunks, all covering the same side of each tree. The north side.

"It knows its way home like a snow goose does," Tobin said.

"Huh?" Wiley slunk up alongside him.

"Look." Tobin pointed a tiny claw straight ahead. "The fungus all grows on the same side of each tree, like it's pointing us in the direction of the spider lair."

"And we can use it to show us the way home," Talia added.

"Yes!" Tobin grinned; this was a lucky break. He looked ahead and spotted a gnarled tree root, twisting half in and half out of the ground—plenty of room for them to squeeze beneath. Perfect for their spider-trailing technique: following under cover. He sprang forward. Right as he did, a whiff of something peculiar crossed his nose.

Another animal.

Danger.

Snake.

"Bolt!" Tobin yelled, focused only on the tree roots and cutting the quickest path to them. His pumped his legs, the rest of the forest becoming a blur. A space between tree root and dirt was in reach, and he dived. Talia and Wiley crashed in behind him. Tobin threw them a sideways glance. All eyes wide, noses sniffing—they smelled it, too.

No one dared move. Tobin braced for an attack. Had the snake noticed them? Had they been upwind? Tobin let out a shaky breath when nothing immediately attacked.

The Arakni they were tracking wasn't as lucky.

A sliver of motion caught Tobin's eye.

There, ahead of them, was the snake. And it struck with reptilian precision at the Arakni, grabbing it with its jaws. The serpent propelled itself to the nearest tree, ramming the startled spider into the bark. The Arakni exploded on impact, its inner goo smearing the tree bark and dribbling down the snake's snout.

With a jerk of its head, the serpent flung the Arakni aside, a glint of green flashing from the snake's eyes. The Arakni's limp body landed with a splat outside their crawl space under the root. The websack rolled free—its inhabitant twitching wildly. Tobin's eyes darted back to the point of attack. The snake was gone.

"The snake's not eating it," Talia whispered.

Tobin shrugged. "Let's hope he just goes away."

A fresh whiff of snake skin, sourer and more pungent than ever before, crossed his nose, and his hopes fizzled. It was close. But where? He didn't dare peek out from beneath the tree root.

But peeking would not be necessary.

A red, fork-shaped tongue skimmed across the ground. A hiss reverberated into the tiny crevice. The fur on Tobin's shoulders bristled. Pressed as far back into the root-covered crawl space as possible, Tobin fought the urge to close his eyes. The serpent's snout slid into view. The scales shone black as raven feathers. It nudged forward, tongue flicking across the threshold of their crawl space. Then it stopped.

Could it reach them? Tobin felt Talia tremble and realized he was shaking, too.

Rule #10: The strategy for the trapped band of rodents is to scatter; better some survive than none.

Scatter.

He and Wiley would easily outrun Talia, leaving her to . . .

No.

Never.

"Wiley, hold on to Talia," Tobin whispered.

Wiley laid a tentative paw on Talia's shoulder. "What are you doing?"

Tobin willed his legs to quit trembling beneath him. "It knows we're here. I'm going to give it something to chase."

nine

TALIA'S EARS DROOPED FLAT. "You can't." She
tried to lunge toward Tobin, but Wiley hugged her close.

Tobin's throat tightened. "Have to."

"Let's just wait until—" Wiley ducked his head just as
the forked tongue flicked dangerously close.

The snake moved. Like a dark cloud passing the sun,
its snout slid across the opening of their crevice. It pushed
and probed. It was looking for a way in.

Tobin swallowed, though his throat felt coated with
creek sand. He looked from Wiley to Talia and spoke
fast. "Listen, Dad and I once watched a garter snake eat
this huge lump of a toad. Dad said the snake wouldn't
need to eat for a week, maybe t-two." Tobin stuttered
at the memory of the slack-jawed snake, swallowing the
toad with its eyes rolled up into its head. . . . "Anyway."

He shook his head. "That snake could sit there for days digesting its last meal, knowing we're pinned in here for whenever it gets hungry again."

The serpent cocked its head. The red tongue flicked low, lapping the dirt a whisker's-width from their paws. The forked tip curled upward, brushing the tree-root canopy.

The snake's tongue was long.

Vulnerable!

Tobin launched. Swiping his front paw over his head, his claws raked the pink, rubbery underside of the snake's tongue. The serpent whipped its head back, injured tongue dangling, and Tobin darted just beneath its jaws. The warm air of a hiss blasted his fur as he bolted toward the nearest bush, just a hare-leap away. But the bush . . . moved. Its limbs squirmed.

It was full of snakes.

Tobin dug his claws into the ground, tried to pivot, but he tumbled forward, rolling straight into a night-mare.

He'd broken the Rules, and now he was going to die.

Snakes of all sizes, in shades of browns, greens, grays, wove through the branches of the bush. Their beady eyes stared down at him. A snake no bigger than a night crawler dropped from a limb and landed beside him, opening its mouth in a silent hiss.

Tobin scrambled to his feet and turned. The big black snake was upon him. He stood frozen, and the forest began to spin. Black dots of panic threatened to blind him. Snakes slithered in closer, from all directions. Dozens of them. Hundreds?

Tobin sat dead center in a ring of squirming, scale-covered serpents. They wove and tightened, creating a self-made barrier, closing in around him. Smaller snakes slid in to fill any gaps left by the bigger ones. Above him, the branches of the bush drooped with the weight of more spying serpents.

But no snakes struck at him. *What are they waiting for?*

The hissing grew louder, vibrating in Tobin's ears. He closed his eyes. Whatever was about to happen, he didn't want to see it.

"Sssuch bravery, from a moussse."

Say what?

Tobin cracked open an eye. A snake covered in indigo-blue scales slid before him, staring down with piercing, golden eyes.

"Huh?" Tobin cleared his throat, letting a tiny squeak escape. *Oh, very nice.*

The corners of the snake's mouth curled. A smile? "Ssso small, yet ssso brave."

Tobin kneaded his paws into the ground, trying to summon the strength to speak. "Who . . . who are you?"

The indigo snake dipped her head. "Questionsss." She spoke slowly, her mouth contorting on each syllable. Her words vibrated in Tobin's ears like there was a bee trapped inside his head.

She turned to the crowd of snakes and spoke in her language. Harsh spitting, hisses, clicks and jaw snaps. Another snake slid forward to join them. Long, but not as thick as the indigo snake, this new serpent glistened black with a clover-green stripe racing down each side. It shook its head then opened its mouth, jaws stretching wide, *impossibly wide.*

Tobin's breath caught in his throat. The serpent's lip scales curled back, showing pointy teeth that curved backward. Teeth perfect for swallowing mice. Even the fur on his feet stood on end.

"Easssy," the indigo snake cooed.

The black snake's jaws snapped shut. The newcomer looked at Tobin and spoke. "Sorry. It's easier to speak rodent-tongue if I stretch my mouth first. My name is Hess."

94

Tobin's jaw dropped open.

Hess cocked his head. "Hello? Am I speaking correctly?" The snake spoke clearly, though his voice carried the same vibrations that tickled Tobin's eardrums.

Tobin nodded quickly. "I . . . I understand you."

Hess tilted his head toward the indigo snake. "This is Queen Hesthpa, ruler of Serpentes. As her chosen interpreter, I speak on her behalf."

Tobin looked from the snake queen back to Hess. *The snake speaks better rodent-tongue than I do.*

Hess continued. "Queen Hesthpa is curious why you and your two friends are following spiders."

Uh-oh. A shiver ran from Tobin's shoulders to tail. They'd been spied on—by *snakes*. "We just happen to be heading in that direction."

"Come now." Hess cocked his head. "No animal accidentally stays in the same proximity as those beasties if they can help it."

Tobin tensed his whole body, hoping it would keep the shaking from his voice. "So what if we were following them?"

Hess raised his chin. "What direction were they heading?"

"Due north." Tobin broke his gaze away from Hess

and looked toward the woods. "The crescent fungus on the trees sprouts on the north side. It seems to point the way."

Queen Hesthpa's gold eyes twinkled. "S-s-ee? I told you mice were sssmart." There was hunger in her eyes. She wanted something, but Tobin was beginning to think it wasn't a mouse-sized meal.

A sudden squeal caught Tobin's attention.

The ring of snakes parted, making way for two serpents. They each held a mouse in their mouths, hanging by the scruffs of their neck.

"Put me down!" Talia was yelling. Wiley looked like a miniature badger, his fur bristling and his teeth snapping through thin air.

So much for the escape plan. Tobin stomped a paw. "What are you two doing here?"

The snakes dropped the mice, who quickly darted beside him.

"What's going on?" Talia asked.

Tobin shook his head, frustration briefly squashing his fear. "I don't know, but I was kind of hoping you two would be long gone. Remember? I run; you guys go the other way?"

"The queen is interested in your journey," Hess

interrupted, then looked directly at Tobin. "Don't be disappointed with your friends. We've had you all surrounded for quite some time. They weren't going anywhere."

Tobin's legs suddenly felt a little wobbly beneath him. "But . . . why?"

"Quesstions," Queen Hesthpa answered.

"Right, we have a partnership to discuss." Hess narrowed his eyes, looking over the three mice. *A partnership?* Tobin's mind was reeling.

"Why don't we start with introductions." The snake continued, "As I've said, my name is Hess. Who are the three of you?"

Talia's jaw dropped. She stared at the talking snake, her wide eyes blinking.

For the first time in his life, Tobin saw his sister speechless.

ten

SO FAR, COOPERATION WAS keeping them alive. Tobin wanted to keep it that way. He cleared his throat and spoke. "I'm Tobin, and this is my sister, Talia, and my best friend, Wiley." Tobin nudged Talia's shoulder.

"Um, hello," said Talia, the word sounding more like a question than a greeting. Her stare traced a path along the long, emerald stripe running down Hess's side.

Hess nodded. "Pleased to meet you."

Tobin swallowed. Trying to keep his cool, he nodded toward the queen. "And this is Snake Queen Hesthpa."

Talia's focus snapped to the blue serpent coiled beside Hess. "A queen?" Talia lowered her voice, leaning toward Tobin. "We should let Camrik know ants and bees aren't the only animals with queens."

Queen Hesthpa raised her head with a regal nod.

"Creaturesss can be ssso sssurprisssing."

"So." Tobin clenched the dirt beneath his paws to steady himself. "What did you mean when you said you had a partnership to discuss?"

Queen Hesthpa swung her head toward Tobin, her movement as fluid as poured water. "I sssaw you sssearching for ssspidersss." Her tongue flicked, brushing Tobin's nose. Her breath reeked of death. "I know what I ssssaw, and I want to know why."

Tobin felt his composure slipping like a stone into the creek mud. Had they broken some serpent Rule about tailing Arakni? "Is it a problem if we're following them?"

The snake queen lifted her head, taking on a more poised appearance. "Hess, exssplain."

The black serpent nodded. "You see, we are curious about the spiders. Over the last few seasons, they've grown more"—Hess paused, his head cocked to the side—"aggressive."

Aggressive enough to bother snakes? The Arakni were becoming more terrifying by the minute. Tobin cleared his throat. "In rodent-tongue, we call the spiders 'Arakni.' And yeah, we're following them. We want to find where they're taking their captives."

Hacking-sounding whispers of *Arakni! Arakni!* rippled

from the snakes, their angry hisses surrounding them in a chorus—the enemy had a name.

"Thessse Arakni." Queen Hesthpa's voice trembled with rage; her long body twitched. "They sssteal my hatchlingsss!"

Talia gasped, and her ears drooped. "The Arakni stole our pinkling, too."

Queen Hesthpa tilted her chin, looking down at Talia. "You shhall passs sssafely."

Tobin's face flushed with heat. Could they possibly walk out of this?

The snake queen spoke to Hess in a flurry of hisses and spits. Hess nodded every few moments. When she finished, she touched Hess's forehead with her chin. Without another glance at the mice, she turned and slithered toward a tangle of fallen branches. Oodles of worm-sized snakes seemed to emerge from under every nearby rock and crevice, gliding alongside the queen. Together they looked like one giant, scale-covered centipede. The remaining snakes slithered off in their own directions.

All but one.

Hess's golden eyes seemed to stare straight through Tobin. "Well, mouse, it seems I'm to accompany you."

The very thought made Tobin's tail twitch. "Wait, you . . . what?"

"The queen is eager to learn the location of the Arakni lair. She is considering relocating our hibernaculum in order to keep our hatchlings safe. She sees potential in a rodent-reptile partnership to gather this information."

Wiley's ears flattened. "Does this partnership include a Do Not Eat clause?"

The scales at the corners of Hess's mouth stretched into a smile. "I will do you no harm. Quite the opposite. I'm an experienced scout, and I can deter some predators—"

"Oh yeah? My brother's a scout, too," Talia interrupted. "And he's very good."

She did not . . .

"Talia, quiet." Tobin shook his head.

"Really, a scout?" said Hess.

The snake looked him up and down, and Tobin knew Hess wanted him to elaborate. His "skills" were the last thing Tobin wanted to talk about. *He'd just led them into snake central!* Not quite the behavior of an experienced scout.

"I'm a weather scout, mostly. I study the different weather cues and smells, and sort of apply it to the Rules of Rodentia. But I'm doing my best to track the Arakni."

"Excellent," said Hess. "I'd like to hear how you three have gotten this far."

Tobin nervously grabbed his tail and began squeezing. "Um, sure."

But before Tobin could say any more, a black snake with a drooping red tongue slithered out from a bush. Tobin recognized the snake who had trapped them under the tree root, and he suddenly wished he could hide from the snake and its injury.

When Hess finished talking to the viper, Hess looked back toward the mice. "Come now, Tobin, was that really necessary?"

Tobin cringed. "I swear, we didn't realize you snakes just wanted to talk."

"Hmm." Hess's forehead scales crinkled. "Well, let's see how bad it is."

Tobin craned his neck to see what Hess inspected on the injured viper.

"Look up," Hess instructed, and the viper lifted its snout skyward. A small welt poked out on the viper's chin.

Tobin took a step back. "I did not do that."

Hess exhaled sharply, looking the viper right in the

eyes. "Go to the hibernaculum, get a mouthful of yarrow leaves under that tongue. It should stop the bleeding and reduce the swelling. Then, spit out the yarrow and rest your chin on it."

The injured snake nodded, then turned its head, baring a lone fang at Tobin before slithering away.

Tobin raised a paw. "I do not know what happened to his chin," he repeated.

"I know." Hess nodded his head. "It was obviously the spider. Err, the Arakni." Hess paused. "You do know that an Arakni hunter can stun prey with a jab from its front leg, don't you?"

Wiley frowned. "It can what?"

"Yes," Hess continued. "There is a sharp tip at the end of an Arakni's front legs. Like a bee's stinger, I suppose. It releases a paralytic venom into its victim.

Wiley looked like he smelled something terrible. "A *what*-a-lytic?"

"Par-a-ly-tic," Hess pronounced slowly. "It renders its smaller-sized prey unable to move. It paralyzes them. For a snake like that one"—Hess jerked his head toward the exiting viper—"it will leave a painful welt."

Wiley stared at the big black snake and drew a deep, slow breath. "Okay. That is good to know. Thank you."

"So, this partnership—" Hess began.

Wiley eyed Tobin. "Can we talk?"

Tobin chewed his lip. Could he just excuse himself for a chat? He almost laughed—almost. In his wildest dreams, this situation was still impossible. And yet, here they were.

"Hess." Tobin looked up. "Could we have a moment? Just to gather our thoughts?"

Gather our thoughts? Tobin cringed. Now I sound like an Eldermouse.

Hess cocked his head, his tongue flicking in and out a few times before finally saying, "I suppose." The snake slithered no more than a hare-leap away and coiled up, his eyes always fixed on the mice.

Wiley spoke in a hushed voice. "So, clearly these snakes aren't big fans of the spiders, either. But travel with one? I don't know."

Talia scratched her head. "I can't believe I'm going to say this, but I think traveling with a snake could have some perks. He can protect us, and anyway, Hess seems sort of nice?"

"Of course he's going to come off that way," Wiley said, eyes rolling. "I've played a lot of jokes on my brother, and most of them start with me smooth-talking him."

Tobin gave his tail a final squeeze. "Exactly," he whispered. "We need to be careful. Once Hess gets whatever he needs from us . . ." Tobin shook his head. "You just never know."

Wiley nodded. "If we ever get too suspicious, we'll bolt. There are ways to ditch a snake, even a big one."

"Especially a big one," Tobin agreed. He looked up into a purple-tinged sky. It had gotten late, and a lone star shone on the horizon. "The Nightbreak Star's already out. We can talk to Hess more on the way. Maybe get a better feel for him."

Wiley and Talia each silently nodded their agreement. It wasn't like they had a lot of choice.

They would have to partner with a serpent.

"Okay, Hess," Tobin called. "We're ready to head out."

The serpent uncoiled and swerved up beside them. "Now perhaps you can fill me in on the beginning of your journey."

"Yeah, sure," Tobin answered. As the snake began to slither onto the Arakni trail, Tobin glanced at the side of Hess's head. Where would the snake's ear hole be? Seeing none, he just began talking, telling the story of their journey thus far. Hess guided them deeper into the woods, flicking his scent-sensitive tongue and lifting his head to nod every few moments, assuring Tobin he was actually listening.

Eventually the snake had a question. "So, tell me about these Rules of Rodentia."

Tobin's forehead scrunched. He forgot for a moment he'd mentioned them to Hess. "Well, I guess I've never really explained them before. We are all just taught growing up to follow the Rules. The Eldermice pass them on to us. They're like a survival guide for rodents."

"Except," Wiley piped up from behind, "Tobin's a whiz with the Rules. He's as good as any Eldermouse. It's like the right Rule for every occasion always just pops into his head."

Hess stopped slithering. "Really?"

Tobin's ears burned. How must this sound to a *snake*? "I don't know. I just really like practicing them, I guess."

"More than that." Talia hopped into the conversation. "Tobin hears a Rule, and it's like stuck in his brain. It's why Tobin likes to stay busy. He said some days the Rules jump around in his skull so hard it's like a chick trying to break out of its shell."

Tobin stopped, sitting up on his haunches. "I told that to Dad!"

Talia's nose crinkled. "I know. I heard you guys talking in the den. I didn't know it was supposed to be some secret thing."

Hess raised his chin. "Tobin, it sounds like you have a gift, and that's fascinating. This will be an interesting partnership, indeed."

Hess turned and continued his slither. Wiley sat up and wiggled his shoulders. Using his best Eldermouse voice, he chimed in, "Indeed, good fellow. Indeed."

Tobin smiled, glad for his friend's humor to relieve his complete and total embarrassment.

Talia.

Tobin glared at his sister. "Please don't tell anyone else that chick-in-egg thing, got it?"

"Fine, but I don't know why you're so embarrassed." Talia dramatically clasped her paws together. "Oh no, poor Tobin! He has a gift, and the Eldermice always talk about how wonderful he is." She spun on her heels and trotted up alongside Hess's head.

Tobin snapped his gaze to Wiley. "What the heck was that?"

Wiley scratched behind his ear as he thought. "I think, maybe, your sister was trying to compliment you, but it sort of veered into awkward territory."

"Just because nothing ever embarrasses her." Tobin shook his head. "Whatever. Let's just hope she sticks to talking about herself instead."

Wiley nodded, and the pair fell in behind Talia, who was happily chatting with Hess about the process of snake-skin shedding.

Traveling snake-style was *very* different. Hess moved like a whisper in the grass. The serpent didn't scurry across the forest floor; he *wove* across it, slithering in curves and making a zigzagging path. Trying to run alongside him was tricky. Hess's head veered back forth. He'd stop suddenly, shoveling his snout around in the forest litter, searching for scents. Then he'd look up and take off again. Each time they passed a shrub, Tobin fought his urge to dive for cover.

Hess knew the dangers of this stretch of forest, reminding Tobin of how he knew the hazards surrounding the Great Burrow. Hess moved them safely around a badger den and had them crawl beneath a leafy vine that stretched across the territory of a nesting hawk.

When they approached a small scattering of rocks, Hess ordered them to stay put beneath a low-hanging pine branch.

"What's he doing?" Wiley whispered.

Tobin shrugged. He watched the snake root around the base of the rock pile, then slither over its top. Hess's probing snout found a gap in the stones, and he disappeared inside.

Talia shook her head. "I hope there's nothing in there."

Tobin couldn't tell if she was worried for Hess's safety or for some poor creature that was about to get ambushed.

Soon enough, Hess emerged from a slit between the stones and ground and jerked his head, beckoning the mice to come over.

Setting all mouse sense aside, Tobin ran toward the snake.

"I've found a place we can rest for the night," Hess said.

"We're stopping?" said Tobin.

Hess nodded. "The hour of the owls and bobcats is near. The best protection I can provide is to hide you."

"But our pinkling needs us now," said Talia. "We can't leave it with those spiders all night!"

A rustle in the treetops sent chills down Tobin's spine. Hess coiled, baring his fangs at the unseen creature above.

Tobin nudged his sister. "Go inside. It's not safe out here."

"But our pinkling is alone," Talia cried, "and probably cold and scared, and needs us."

Hess spoke to her, his gaze never leaving the treetop. "Your pinkling needs you to live through the night."

Hopping in front of her, Tobin spoke to Talia nose to nose. "Tal, there's *something* in that tree, and we need to get our tails inside."

Tears began to rim her eyes, but she turned and scurried between the stones.

Tobin followed, and Wiley and Hess slipped in after them. The interior of the rock pile was roomier than Tobin expected, probably big enough for a family of weasels.

Talia wedged herself into a crook, looking miserable. Her ears sagged. Even her whiskers drooped.

Hess circled around, rubbing his snout along the opening. Tobin smelled the musty scent of snake seep from Hess's glands. "This should give pause to any predators sniffing around."

Wiley's eyelids fluttered and he coughed. "I'll say."

The snake odor hit Tobin's nose like musk and sour fruit. He swiped his paw over his muzzle. "Whoa."

If Talia smelled it, she didn't show it. She looked down at the floor, ignoring all the stares floating in her direction. After the way he spoke, Tobin knew he needed to say something to her. And it'd better be nice. He walked over and sat beside her.

"Tal," he said. "I know you're worried about the pinkling. I am, too, but I'm also worried about you. And Wiley."

Talia sniffed. Her eyes were still fixed on the floor.

Tobin continued. "Hess knows these woods the best and I think we need to trust him. That noise in the trees could have been an owl or a lynx."

Talia finally raised her head, defiance still glinting in her eyes. "Oh? It also could've just been a squirrel flicking a flea off its tail."

His own laugh caught Tobin unprepared; it filled the tiny cavern, followed by Wiley's chuckling.

Talia's cheeks scrunched as she fought a smile. "Well, it could have!"

Wiley rose up onto his hind legs, his front claws outstretched. "But what if it was a rabid squirrel, Tal? Heeere, little mouseling."

The mice laughed harder, and Tobin looked over to Hess. The big snake seemed amused at their spectacle, his head cocked to the side.

The smile disappeared from Talia's face when she met Hess's gaze. "Can you promise our pinkling will be all right tomorrow?"

Hess regarded her for a moment before he spoke. "Remember, Talia, the spiders are only harvesting food right now, not eating it. I believe we could reach the lair by midday tomorrow."

Tobin swallowed the lump that suddenly sprang up in his throat. The Arakni lair. How many spiders lived in a lair? At least they traveled with a weapon now—a snake strong enough to pummel spiders with a flick of his head. If Hess kept his word, that is.

Either way, Hess's comment seemed to make Talia feel a little better. She curled up beside Tobin and shut her eyes. "Tobin," she whispered. "Mom and Dad are okay, right? I mean, the spider grabbed our pinkling, but it couldn't hurt Mom and Dad. Could it?"

Tobin settled in beside her. He'd avoided thinking about their parents since they'd crossed the tree bridge, only thinking on them enough to formulate a loose theory. "I'm sure they're fine, Tal. I think Mom was probably resting and the spider snuck up and snatched the pinkling somehow. I'm sure they'll tell us when we get home."

"That makes sense." She wrapped her tail snugly around her body.

Tobin rested his head on his paws. He peeked up at the snake on guard duty. He wondered if Hess would sleep, or watch them all night with those unblinking, golden eyes. As he drifted off to sleep, he realized drowsily he never thought he'd be grateful for a snake's company.

eleven

TOBIN COULD HAVE SWORN he'd just fallen asleep when Talia's twitching paws poked him awake. He cracked his eyelids open. The first beams of sunlight were pushing through tiny gaps in the rocky fortress, spreading a wave of warmth across his chilly nose and paws. Talia was still sleeping curled next to him; Wiley beside her. Hess sat coiled, gazing in the direction of the only crevice big enough for a possible invader. Had he sat like that all night? Even if they didn't have eyelids, snakes had to sleep sometime.

Tobin rose, trying not to disturb the others. He stretched his hind legs just as a yawn escaped him. Hess's glossy eyes flickered to life. Though it was hard to read the reptile's face, Tobin thought his new travel companion looked glad someone else was up.

With a steadying breath, Tobin approached their

serpent guide and spoke in a hushed voice. "Well, if you were going to eat us, you probably would have last night."

Hess smiled. "You're right. But I pledged to keep you safe."

A thousand questions tumbled in Tobin's mind, and maybe because he was still groggy, one managed to tumble right out. "But do you *want* to eat us?"

Hess's eyes stretched wide. "It's much harder to eat someone after you've been formally introduced, *Tobin*."

"Right. Sorry." Tobin cringed. "I don't introduce myself to grubs before chowtime, either."

Hess tilted his head. "I suppose I'm the first snake you've ever talked to. Naturally you'll have questions."

Tobin nodded. "I'll try not to make them stupid ones."

Hess made a coughing, hissy sound—a laugh? "It's all right, Tobin. But may I ask you a question?"

"Sure," Tobin answered.

"What do your Rules of Rodentia say about leading rescue missions to save pinklings?"

"Oh." Tobin scratched his head. "Well, there's not really anything, specifically, about that." *Quite the opposite, in fact.*

"I thought maybe not," said Hess.

"But . . ." Tobin stared at the ground, searching for the answer. "Wiley always says the Rules are open for

114

interpretation." Tobin glanced at his friend, still sleeping beside Talia. "I think looking out for the good of the colony also means looking out for my mom."

Hess raised his chin. "Your mom?"

"It's just . . ." Tobin ran a paw across the gravelly ground, feeling the particles weave between his paw pads, until finally the words spilled out in a rush. "Last year my mom had a pinkling, but it was born asleep and never woke up, ever."

Hess's mouth opened, but no words came out.

Tobin flicked his tail forward into his paws and squeezed before continuing. "I don't want her to be sad like that again. Not ever again."

Hess slowly nodded, the scales on his forehead seeming to crease with concern. "Tobin, do you have any other brothers or sisters at home?"

"No, it's just me and Talia. Why?"

Hess's eyes focused on something Tobin couldn't see. It was a faraway look, the kind someone gets when they're preoccupied with the thoughts in their mind. "All of your parents' children are here then, across the creek, away from home," Hess said.

Tobin nodded in silence, the gravity of Hess's thoughts sinking deep.

Hess continued, "You should probably wake Talia and

Wiley now. And, rest assured, they are also off my menu."

Tobin let the smallest smidge of a smile creep on his muzzle. Hess had a sense of humor.

Inching up to his companions, Tobin gently nudged Talia. "Hey, time to get up."

She stretched and yawned as she rose. "I'm up."

Tobin poked Wiley with his tail. "C'mon Wiley, rise and shine."

Wiley's eyes sprang open and he bolted upright, his gaze fixed on the black serpent.

"Easy, Wiley, it's just Hess," said Tobin, daring to rest a paw on Wiley's shoulder. "Easy."

Wiley's stare lingered a moment longer before drifting to Tobin. "Oh yeah." He blinked and shook his head. "Spiders. We're chasing spiders." His claws loosened from the floor.

Hess's voice vibrated around the rocky den. "I'm going to take a look outside. I'll signal you if it's safe to follow."

The snake slithered through the opening, only the tip of his tail remaining inside. The scaly point rested still for a few moments before it twitched. Left. Right. Around.

Wiley squinted. "Think that's the signal?"

"I'd say so," said Tobin. He poked his nose outside, then scampered alongside Hess's long body. By the time he reached the serpent's snout, Tobin could see there was a slight complication. "Little foggy this morning, huh?"

"Yes," Hess said between flicks of his tongue. "Remember, stay close and stay quiet. The fog isn't ideal, but time is of the essence. The Arakni scent is still strong."

Tobin nodded, then looked behind him. "Hey Tal, Wiley—stay close to Hess. We need to travel through the fog."

Talia nodded immediately, but Wiley hesitated. Tobin knew why, and exactly what his friend was thinking:

Rule #11: Fog can settle, and fog can roll; wait for the roll before you go.

Without question, this fog wasn't moving anywhere, and they should stay put until it did.

But.

Tobin looked to Wiley. "Not only is the Arakni scent still strong, we also have to get to the pinkling sooner than later, right?"

Wiley cocked his head. "You know, Tobin, if we need to do a few things snake-style this trip, I get it. Really."

"Okay." Tobin wiped a paw across his forehead. Here they were, on the biggest trek of their lives, and he found himself bending, breaking, and twisting the Rules.

"Tobin." Talia stepped in front and faced him snout to snout. "Let's face it, what works for weather scouting may not work for rescue scouting."

Tobin's ears pricked up at the thought. "Is that what we're doing? Rescue scouting?"

Talia smiled and shrugged. "Something like that."

"That's a new one." Tobin nodded slowly. "Maybe you can talk the Eldermice into rescue scouting when we get back."

"Maybe," Talia called as she crept up near Hess's head. "I think we're all set," she said to the serpent. Tobin fell in line behind Talia, and Wiley stepped behind him.

Hess pulled ahead, beginning his swerve across the foggy forest floor. Above, many regular morning noises filled the air; birds called, squirrels loudly scampered through the branches, and somewhere in the distance a woodpecker thrummed its beak against a tree trunk looking for breakfast. Tobin thought for a moment about the woodpecker, not much bigger than a robin, yet the thunderous noise they made hammering their beaks against the trees amazed him. They seemed to be drifting closer to where the woodpecker worked, as the percussion of its beak rapping on bark felt like it was tapping directly on his eardrums.

The fur along Tobin's spine suddenly rose. He thrust his paw—claws out—into Hess's side. They all froze. A change . . . *something* changed.

He sniffed, slow, shallow breaths. A new odor. It was faint, but undeniable. And another odor now, too, as Hess swelled up, emitting his own warning scent. So slightly, Tobin turned his head from Hess, and he caught a stronger whiff. Canine. *Fox.*

Tobin's gaze zeroed in on a bush roughly two hare-leaps away. Through the haze of fog, an orange-and-black muzzle seemed to materialize between the leaves.

It sees us. Do they see it? Tobin averted his eyes quickly to see Talia in front of him, her head tilted toward the fox. She saw. What would the fox do? A trail of mice alongside a large snake. Just how hungry was it?

They didn't have to wait long to find out.

twelve

TOBIN DIDN'T REALIZE HOW far a fox could jump. When it sprang, they scattered, and only a puff of dirt remained. The fox landed squarely where they'd been. Hess side-slithered to avoid a direct blow from its paw, but the fox spun and kicked out with its hind legs. From the corner of his eye, Tobin saw Hess sail across the forest floor and land in a pile of rotting branches.

Tobin dove into a thicket of boxwood, squeezing between the densest tangles near the base. He could hear Talia huffing, pushing her way in behind him. He squirmed forward, making room for her and Wiley. Pressing himself low to where the branch stems became roots, Tobin stopped. Talia slid into the small groove beside him. Tobin waited, one breath, then two . . . but no Wiley.

He nudged Talia. She looked at him, puzzlement clear on her face.

A soft whine filtered through the branches, followed by a yipping bark. The fox chattered—but not directly outside their shrub. Talia leaned into Tobin. She barely breathed the words, "Where is Wiley?"

Tobin shook his head and reached, grabbing hold of a stem. He whispered back, "Going to look. Stay here. *Pleeeease.*"

A flash of frustration crossed Talia's face, but she nodded nonetheless.

With a quick nod, Tobin ascended the gnarled, twisty branches until the leafy foliage thinned and he could see the scene unfolding.

His heart sank. Wiley, what were you thinking?

Clinging to the very tip of a wispy pine bough, Wiley was holding on for dear life. The tree stood no taller than a grown moose, and Wiley clung only inchworms out of easy reach for the fox. The fox's tail swooshed excitedly across the forest floor. It yipped, whined, then jumped— its jaws snapping. Wiley swung himself to the opposite side of the treetop, just avoiding the deadly bite. The skinny tree wobbled and swayed. It was only a matter of time before the fox connected. Wiley was sitting fox bait.

For a fleeting second, Tobin considered that maybe Wiley had done this on purpose, maybe as a decoy so he and Talia could escape? Like he himself had done before with the snakes. Now Tobin knew why they hadn't left him behind, either.

The fox launched itself again, and the *crunch-crunch* snapping of its jaws shot fissures of fear deep through Tobin's bones. He looked around wildly. What could he do? And *where* was Hess? Hurt? Fled? That fox had kicked the snake pretty hard. . . .

A flutter of feathers caught Tobin's eye, and he looked up.

Sludge.

A young falcon had noticed the commotion and landed on a nearby branch, watching intently. Tobin's tail swished behind him. "Oh, you have got to be kidding," he muttered. Then a thought: *two predators, two mice.*

Can't think; just act. Funneling his nervous energy into his legs, Tobin rocked forward, then back, forward, back, and jumped.

He jettisoned toward the forest floor, calling a loud *tchirr!* for good measure. The young falcon, already on alert, couldn't resist the bait. It stretched out its wings and swooped.

Tobin's paws scrambled the moment he hit the ground.

His claws cut through dirt until he was running—running directly toward the fox.

The flurry of activity grabbed the fox's attention, and it whirled around, leaving the spindly tree and Wiley behind it.

Tobin locked his gaze on the startled canine. The sound of the wind rushing through the falcon's feathers filled his ears, and the shadow of its talons bloomed across the ground.

The fox lifted its head, seeing the bird swooping close, dangerously close—

The fox stumbled backward, bumping into the tree, and Tobin shot right between its legs, sailing past the tree and into a bramble of bushes.

He heard the collision behind him; first a soft thud of feathers hitting fur. Then screeches, snarls, as the two predators tangled.

Tobin wedged himself into a crevice between shrub root and ground and froze. He shut his eyes, concentrating on breathing and slowing his thrumming heart.

Then a whisper from behind: "Wow, that was something."

The noise nearly sent Tobin shooting up through the shrub and into the stratosphere.

"Wiley," Tobin scolded in the harshest whisper that

he dared. "Don't sneak up like that—and shush!"

The two sat in silence. In the following long moments, they heard a crunching sound, followed by the sounds of paw pads trotting away; the fox had departed.

They remained sitting in silence for a few long moments. A soft *tchirr!* from above broke them from their trance.

"Talia," Tobin whispered.

Cautiously, the two crept out from the denseness of the brush and looked up, toward the source of the call.

There, on the lowest limb of a nearby spruce, sat Talia. Nestled into a trio of pine cones, she was almost invisible. She nodded, and Tobin nodded back. Then Talia jerked her head to the side, and Tobin figured she must want them to follow her.

Spotting a scrap of bark near the base of the spruce tree, Tobin and Wiley darted to Talia's tree and wiggled beneath, waiting. Tobin *tchirr*ed.

A scent—at first scary, but then familiar—crossed his nose. Swallowing a lump in his throat, Tobin peeked out from beneath the scratchy scrap of wood. He watched as Talia shimmied down the tree trunk and hopped off, landing right beside the onyx-colored serpent. Tobin's breath caught in his throat as he watched his sister walk over to, and then lean into, the big snake.

"She's getting attached," Tobin quietly observed.

Wiley sidled up alongside him. "Aren't you?" His voice was unusually sincere.

Tobin's stare was fixed on Hess and his sister. "I don't know that we should. Where was he after the fox appeared?"

Wiley shrugged. "He took a pretty good hit from that fox. Besides, you didn't really give him a chance to do anything. You pulled off your stunt so quickly. Which was awesome, by the way."

"Oh, thanks." Tobin tapped a claw on the dirt. "Well, Hess is all we've got for now anyway, right?"

Wiley chuckled. "That's the spirit. C'mon, we need to get moving," he said, and he scampered the hare-leap distance to Hess and Talia.

"Right," Tobin answered to no one in particular. He followed Wiley, catching up in time to hear the tail end of Talia's recap.

"And then," Talia said, eyes wide, "Tobin runs right through the fox's legs, and the falcon crashed straight into that orange fleabag."

Hess turned his head to look at him, and Tobin felt like the snake's golden eyes were staring right into his soul.

125

"How, Tobin," Hess asked, "did you ever devise a plan so quickly?"

Tobin scratched his head. "I don't really know—"

"And without fear," Hess interrupted. "Or panic! Why, that fox sent me flying end over end, and here you were, dealing with the situation on your own."

Tobin looked down, finding it hard to speak directly to the gushing snake. "Well, not totally without fear, and not alone, either." He looked to Wiley. "Did you run up that tree so we could escape?"

Wiley's cheeks puffed up with air and he shrugged. "I figured if I bought us a little time you'd figure something out."

Hess snorted. "I'm very impressed."

"Yup, we mice are full of surprises," Wiley said with a grin. "Why, just yesterday I found out Tobin snuck out of his den."

Talia wriggled her nose. "Not exactly the same thing, Wiley."

Wiley patted Tobin on the shoulder. "I'm just saying, there's a mouse with the spine of a badger in there."

"Stop it, Wiley," Tobin pleaded, wanting to get the attention off himself, though soon a very serious thought came rushing forward. *The pinkling.* "We need to get moving."

"Absolutely." Hess nodded, the smallest hint of a smile remaining on his face. "Still, impressive work." Hess raised his head high, and Tobin saw with a cringe the claw marks from where he'd been slapped by the fox.

"Onward." And with that, Hess slid forward, directly through a pile of falcon feathers. Between flicks of his tongue, the serpent spoke. "Remember, stay close and stay quiet."

Tobin nodded, falling in line. The putrid Arakni scent still clung to the forest brush, and they followed it. They wove through thick grasses and weeds and over thistle brushes, and they even passed by a dueling pair of pheasants, until a deep gorge that sliced through the forest floor brought them to stop.

Tobin ducked beneath a patch of ferns, of which half the boughs hung limply over the ledge. Huddling beneath the green canopy, they stared into the canyon below.

"Huh," said Wiley, "it sort of looks like there used to be a creek here, and someone forgot to put water in it."

Hess's long neck dipped over the ridge. "The Arakni trail leads to this ledge." Hess looked at Tobin. "Which is no problem for a spider. Or even a mouse."

"But for you"—Tobin peered across the gorge—"this could be tough."

The climb out the other side looked steep—a sharp incline of crumbly sand, dirt, and clumps of roots. Great for climbers with paws, claws, or wings. None of which Hess had.

Talia sniffed the air breezing up from the gorge. "I don't smell anything dangerous. Maybe just the three of us should cross for now, just to check out the other side."

"No," Hess answered quickly. "Any number of predators could be hiding in ambush, waiting upwind. I can get down easy enough. I'll go with you at least that far."

Wiley's ears flattened. "But then what? We're not gonna leave you stranded down there."

"We'll all cross together," said Tobin, "and we'll find a way out. Together."

Hess nodded. "I'll go first. Stay alert. Let me know if you see any troublemakers."

"Will do." Tobin raised his chin, trying to keep a brave face when really it felt like vines had crept up him and were pulling at his guts. Maybe courting danger came as naturally to Hess as shedding his snake skin, but that was far from Tobin's mentality. "Be careful, everyone."

Hess dipped his head into the gorge and looked back, flashing a small grin. "This probably won't be pretty." Hess lowered himself, gradually at first, the scales on his belly expanding and contracting with his flexing muscles. Tobin fought to keep his eyes on the gorge, not on his friend.

His friend.

Could they be friends? No. That would be ridiculous. Right?

Hess slipped. The bulk of his front half finally pulled him completely off the ledge. Tobin cringed when Hess half skidded, half rolled down the side of the ravine.

Tobin's ears pricked. Twigs snapped and pebbles rolled as Hess fell. Birds and insects went silent; Hess's tumultuous arrival in the gorge was no secret.

Hess finally thumped to a stop against a clump of weeds, then he quickly slithered to a boulder jutting up from the canyon floor. He coiled his body, baring his fangs defensively.

"Ouch," Talia whispered.

Tobin stared in the direction of Hess, but the snake wasn't his focus; the area surrounding the snake was his concern. Any movement could indicate an attacker.

A leaf blew across the gorge floor.

Roots dangling down the gorge walls swayed in the breeze.

Then, a dragonfly flitted off its sheltered perch.

And that was that. The hum of insect life filled the air. No fox or badger charged forth to try and make a meal of Hess.

The snake slid away from the rock. "Come down, and hurry straight to me."

Tobin met eyes with his sister. "Got it, Tal? Hightail it, right to Hess."

She nodded, and Tobin looked to Wiley.

Wiley wriggled his brow fur. "See ya, slugs." And with a burst of dust he sprang off the ledge.

Had there been a gust of wind, every dirt particle would have stuck in Tobin's wide eyes. "It's not a race," he yelled to Wiley's back end.

Talia pounced off her perch with a giggle. Tobin dived after her, his claws digging into the gravelly slope. It took one heartbeat to find his footing, and another to spot Talia. He followed behind, matching her paw for paw. Bounding, scrambling, and finally leaping off a notch of root, Tobin slid to a stop beside Hess.

The snake cocked his head. "You all have no trouble getting around, do you?"

Wiley rubbed a paw against his chest. "You should see us at the creek bed back home."

Talia raised her chin. "May be small, but don't blink

twice, 'cause you'll never catch the creek-side mice." She quoted an old mouse tale.

Hess bowed his head. "It goes without saying, your technique for getting down was far superior to mine." He slithered atop the boulder and stretched his neck high, surveying their surroundings.

For all his whiskers, Tobin wondered if the snake was practically daring any creature watching to come out.

"Snake's not scared of much, is he?" Wiley said quietly to Tobin.

"Nope," said Tobin. "And it's starting to make me nervous."

"I know." Talia nodded. "I'm really glad he's helping us, but what if something happens to him?"

Wiley snorted. "Like getting stuck in this gorge?"

"We'll find a way to get him out," said Tobin, although sitting in the bottom of the gorge *did* make the climb out look even steeper. A smattering of dirt falling into the crevice caught his attention, and he looked up.

A dirty, white, fur-covered snout hung over the ridge. It sniffed, bobbing up and down. The creature dangled by a hairless tail wrapped tightly around the base of a sapling.

A possum.

"Wedge yourselves beneath the boulder," Hess ordered.

Tobin scurried to the sliver of space where the boulder met the ground, cramming beside Talia and Wiley. As close as they sat, Tobin swore he could feel all three of their heartbeats racing.

Hess's hiss echoed from above. A wet sound, like the spray of water hitting boulders in the creek rapids. The possum answered with its own growl, a strange, guttural noise. They did this back and forth, the most terrifying conversation Tobin could imagine.

Clearly curiosity was getting the better of Talia. "What's happening?" she called.

"Hmm? Oh, this possum is trying to frighten me off," Hess muttered, sounding very annoyed. "Leaving you three sitting here, ripe for the picking."

"Ah, sludge, Hess." Wiley shook his head and called up, "Possums are bat-scat bizarre. Try giving it a good scare. Maybe it'll play dead."

After another series of snake and possum hisses and growls, Hess answered, "This one's quite a brute, Wiley. I'm not sure it would play possum for me. I think you're all just going to have to join me up here."

Talia's head snapped up. "Excuse me?"

"Just climb up, stay close, and hopefully it'll get the message that we're—well, a pack of some kind."

Wiley flicked his tail in circles. "This possum could call *us* all bat-scat bizarre. What do you think, Tobin?"

"Well . . ." Tobin paused as the tug-of-war played out in his mind. Trust Hess and sit out in the open, exposed? It's not like Hess slithered off after getting thumped by that fox; surely he wouldn't ditch them over a grumpy possum? "Let's try it," Tobin said, and he stepped from beneath the rock. He pulled himself atop the boulder. The moment the possum laid eyes on him, it tilted its upside-down head and huffed.

Hess raised himself high, balancing almost half the length of his body straight up in the air. His lip scales curled back, showing jagged teeth. He cracked his mouth open. It opened, wider and wider. Impossibly wide—like *his lower jaw might drop clear to the ground* wide.

"Tobin, look away!"

He heard Talia cry out to him, but he couldn't look away. The gross fascination doubled when the smell of death wafted from Hess's mouth to Tobin's nostrils.

"Close your eyes, Tobin!"

The fangs, the smell of death—Tobin's legs wobbled. *Uh-oh.*

He'd contracted Rodent Panic.

Rule #20: When all cues point toward your impending death, embrace the numbness of Rodent Panic for an easier demise.

Like his bones had been replaced with molasses, Tobin slumped to the boulder. His breath came in short gasps. *This. Isn't. Happening . . .*

Tobin tried lifting his head, but it felt rooted to the ground.

A pair of paws clamped over his eyes, shutting his eyelids.

"Listen to my voice, forget the other stuff. *Tchirr, tchirr. Tchirr, tchirr.*"

Talia's voice. Tobin concentrated, hard.

Tchirr, tchirr. Tchirr, tchirr.

A tingle spread through his body, like the prickle of his paw waking up if he'd sat on it too long.

"Snap out of it, birdbrain."

Ah. Wiley decided to chime in.

Tobin drew long, steady breaths. *C'mon, body! Let's move.*

His nose twitched. Then his paws. With great effort, he tucked his chin, making sure his eyes looked down, and he cracked his eyelids open. Talia was beside him, her eyes shut tight and her paws kneading his shoulder.

"I'm coming around," Tobin croaked.

"Good," Talia said breathlessly between *tchirr*s. "Hess is putting on quite a show—*tchirr, tchirr*—and we have no business watching it."

Peeking from nearly shut eyes, Tobin searched for Wiley.

His friend sat perched beside Hess's tail, so Tobin opened his eyes farther.

Of course, Wiley looked anything but scared—his fur stood puffed out on end, making him appear twice his size. Wiley snarled and snapped at the possum. Tobin curled his own lips back, which helped make his own fur puff up. Wiley might truly feel feisty, but Tobin could try to fake it (as long as he didn't actually look at Hess or the possum).

Rule #12: Whether you feel brave or not, going through the motions can trigger an empowering response.

Tobin growled. He thrashed his tail. Instantly, his blood pumped quicker. His legs prickled with energy. "Tal, start growling," he said to his sister.

If this possum wanted a fight, it was going to get one.

thirteen

USING A TAIL THAT looked a lot like a giant earthworm, the possum pulled its dangling body back onto the ridge. There it crouched, resting its wiry-furred muzzle on its paws, watching them.

Tobin heard a *snap!* And glimpsing through half-closed eyes, he saw Hess's jaws clamp back together.

Never taking his stare off the nosy nuisance perched on the ridge above, Hess spoke. "Tobin, climb onto my back."

Tobin's growl fizzled to a low rumble. "What did you say?"

"We need to move out of this possum's territory before it thinks it really has something to fight for."

Wiley reared onto his hind legs, inspecting the snake's back. "There's not really much to hold on to up there."

"Just dig your claws in," said Hess. "My scales are thick. I want to keep my eyes on the possum. If you're up there, I know you're safe."

Talia's whiskers quivered. "I'll get on!" She scrambled up Hess's side, disappearing on his back. The possum's ivory fangs chattered; it clearly did not approve of the strange scene below.

"No one will believe this back home," Tobin said before leaping onto Hess's back. Landing just behind his sister, he gasped seeing how her claws were pressed deep into Hess's scales.

"He doesn't seem to mind," she said quickly. "Honest. He didn't twitch or anything."

Wiley landed behind him, and Tobin flattened his ears. "Dig in, I guess." Tobin's claws sank into the scaly texture, and Talia was right—Hess didn't even flinch.

The snake's attention was still on the possum. Hess called back, "Are you all set?"

Tobin wriggled his nose, then his back end, adjusting his balance. "I guess so."

"Here we go," said Hess.

The movement was not what Tobin expected. Hess slid backward, dropping his back end off the boulder first. Tobin thrashed his tail, tweaking his balance. A nervous laugh flittered from Talia as she adjusted her grip. But they stayed on.

"Sludge, Tobin!" said Wiley. "Watch your tail."

"I couldn't help it," Tobin said.

The possum stomped its paw. Its black eyes burned, mad with confusion.

"Calm yourself, twigs-for-brains," Hess muttered, slithering to the far wall of the gorge. "We'll move faster if you three keep your eyes on our friend up there while I get us across."

"Got it," answered Talia.

With Talia and Wiley both on possum watch, Tobin looked ahead. He wanted to make sure Hess was looking for a route they could *all* take out of the gorge.

They slithered around a curve in the gorge, and for a moment, Tobin enjoyed the smooth, swerving glide of riding atop a snake. *If we could do this for fun sometime . . .*

Tobin shook his head. The pinkling. Getting Hess out of the ravine. Not a good time for silly thoughts.

"Possum's gone," Wiley announced. "Climbed back up its tree."

"About time," said Hess.

About a frog's-leap up the canyon wall, a puff of dust caught Tobin's eye. He craned his head to the side. "Hess, look up."

Again—a splay of sand spurted from between two exposed tree roots. When the sand settled, Tobin could see an opening on the wall of the canyon between the roots.

Hess stopped and swung his head back to look for the possum.

"Look." Tobin whispered. "Something's digging between those roots. Watch."

They waited. First came the sound of claws—large claws—on packed earth.

Scritch-scritch-scritch.

Soon a few pebbles fell down the bank, then a cloud of sand and dirt flew through the air.

Talia loosened her grip from Hess's hide. "I can climb up there and take a look."

"Wait." Tobin thumped his paw on her tail. "Not alone. Could be a rabbit hole, but it could also be a badger."

"It's not too far up." Hess stretched his neck. "I might be able to take a look."

"No offense, Hess." Wiley hopped off the serpent. "But you might scare the tail off whatever's in there, and we only want to talk to it."

Another pitch of rubble. Tobin leaped, clinging to the dirt ridges of the wall. Wiley and Talia followed. They remained still, listening for the burrowing creature.

Scritch-scritch-scritch.

Tobin started climbing. "Get to the side before we're dumped on."

Another wave of sand and pebbles flew from the dugout. Tobin sniffed. There was a musky scent, but not heavy like a badger or fox. The creature shuffled away—this was a rodent for sure, but Tobin couldn't tell what sort.

"I'll go," Wiley whispered.

Tobin nodded and watched Wiley slink into the opening all the rubble had been flying out of. A few heartbeats later, Wiley chattered his teeth, calling them up.

Tobin and Talia scaled the roots edging the entrance, and Hess raised his head high. Wiley sat on the lip of the opening, grinning. "Good news. No, *great* news."

"What?" Talia said.

"We have a woodchuck in here," said Wiley. "He's gone back down the corridor, but I got a good look at his rear end, and this is a definitely a woodchuck burrow."

"Yes! That's perfect," said Tobin.

Hess looked from mouse to mouse. "I'm definitely missing something here. What's so great about woodchucks?"

"Woodchucks eat grass and clover, which means

these tunnels"—Tobin pointed to the gaping hole beside him—"have to lead up."

"Yes," Talia chimed, "if we use these tunnels, we can all get out of this gorge."

Tobin perched on the tunnel ridge beside Wiley. Talia followed, and they all gazed into the woodchuck burrow. It was about two hare-leaps deep before it cranked to the right.

Scritch-scritch-scritch. The woodchuck was coming.

Tobin cleared his throat. "Now all we have to do is introduce ourselves."

fourteen

TOBIN BRUSHED THE DIRT off his head and swiped the dust from his whiskers. Climbing beneath a tunnel excavation project was dirty business, and he wanted to make a good impression. "What should we say?"

Wiley shrugged. "Let's just tell him to back up a minute, because we have a snake coming through."

Talia flattened an ear. "That's not very nice."

"So?" said Wiley. "What if we ask nice and he says no?"

"Hang on," Tobin said. Splashes of dirt pitched into the corridor from around the bend. The woodchuck was getting close with its next load of debris. "I have an idea, just let me talk."

"Fine," Talia and Wiley answered together.

"And Hess, you stay low." Clearing his throat, Tobin took another step, deeper into the tunnel. "Hello?"

The digging claws stopped scraping. Loud sniffing

sounds echoed down the passage. Tobin took a deep breath. "Sorry to bother you, we just have a quick question."

A snort. Paw stomps.

Wiley stepped back. "It's gonna trample us."

Tobin shook his head and called out tried again. "We don't mean any harm."

Tobin never thought a creature with that much bulk could move so fast. The woodchuck darted around the bend, stopping just a frog's-leap in front of them.

Talia sprang back, grasping a dangling root outside the entrance.

"Wait, wait," Tobin yelled. He held out his paw to the woodchuck.

The woodchuck narrowed its eyes and lowered its head. Tobin caught its scent; definitely a boar, and the broadest-shouldered woodchuck he'd ever seen.

"Sorry to bother you." Tobin tried speaking slow and steady, but his thrumming heart made it difficult. "I was just hoping my friends and I could use your tunnels to climb out of this gorge."

The woodchuck's nose twitched as he sniffed them suspiciously. "What ya say?"

Feeling a little more confident they wouldn't be trampled, Tobin asked again. "My name's Tobin. We'd just like to climb topside, with your permission."

"Huh." The woodchuck shifted his weight, eyeing him suspiciously. "Tobin, eh? What are ya, lazy? Yer a mouse. Climb the wall outside. And yer friends, too. Yer all climbers, right?"

"Mostly," Tobin said. "Except one of our friends is having a little trouble."

The woodchuck squinted, looking at Wiley, then to the still-dangling Talia. "Rah! You look spry enough to me."

"Well," said Tobin, "our friend is still down there. He can climb up to your den, but not much farther."

"Is he hurt?"

"No," said Tobin, "he's a snake."

The woodchuck's jaw dropped. He stammered, "Are—Are you diseased? Got some parasite living in yer brain? Disturb my work for nonsense—"

Tobin shook his head. "Please! I promise, um . . . What's your name?"

The woodchuck settled back on his haunches. "Hubbart."

"Hubbart." Tobin spoke quickly. "Just let us through, and the snake will do you a huge favor."

"You," Hubbart huffed, "are crazier than a two-beaked blackbird."

Wiley snorted, seeming amused with the whole situation.

"Just hear me out," Tobin said. "If you let us pass, our snake friend—a large snake—can mark his scent over your tunnel entrances. It's powerful stuff, enough to deter more than a few predators."

Hubbart rested his head on his paw. "Yes, that would be quite a lucky thing—*if* I believed you."

"Let me show you."

"All right, mouse," said Hubbart, rolling his paw in the air. "Show me how this charade ends. Show me your snake friend."

Tobin stepped to the rim of the tunnel. "Hess, can you come up—*slowly*—and say hello?"

Hess slithered against the canyon wall and looked up, his gold eyes twinkling like stars against a black sky. "I can make it," he answered.

"He's coming." Tobin looked up to Talia. "Better get in here and make room."

Talia swung and dropped from her root, landing back inside the tunnel. She skittered to Hubbart. "I'm Talia."

"Charmed," Hubbart replied.

Tobin and Wiley stepped back as the black tip of the serpent's snout rose into view.

"Rah!" Hubbart gasped. The fur on his nose stood

straight up. "What is this? How can it be?"

Hess's head crested into the entrance and he rested his jaws on the floor.

Hubbart began to tremble.

"Don't be scared, Hubbart!" Talia hopped beside Hess's jaws, placing a paw on his cheek. "See? He won't hurt you, we promise."

"It can't be," the woodchuck whispered.

"So, Hess," Tobin began quickly, "I was telling Hubbart—this is Hubbart, by the way—if he lets us use his tunnels, you'll mark the entrances with your snake scent."

Hess snorted. Tobin recognized it as Hess's laugh, but that knowledge did Hubbart little good. The woodchuck flinched, a low rumble sounding from his chest.

"Talia, why don't you and Wiley go on ahead with Hubbart? I'll wait here for Hess to climb in and do his work."

Talia stepped in front of the woodchuck. "I've never seen a woodchuck den."

Hubbart blinked, looking to the little mouseling in front of his nose. He sighed. "Oh, what the hay. Let's go."

The bulky woodchuck shuffled backward and slipped around the bend, Talia and Wiley following.

"Interesting idea, Tobin," said Hess.

146

"Oh, yeah." Tobin batted away the dust on his whiskers. "Thanks for going along. Talia really didn't want us to bully our way through, so I thought this might smooth things a bit."

"You're good at that. Finding the compromise," said Hess.

Tobin laughed. "Am I?"

"Yes." Hess smiled. "Rubbing a scent gland certainly beats having to wrestle past a pudgy woodchuck." Hess reared his head and rubbed his cheek along the stubbly entrance, leaving the strong scent of snake on the gravel.

"Hope that's not too uncomfortable," said Tobin.

Hess swiped his other gland along the bottom ridge. "It doesn't bother me at all. Now stand back, I'm going to need some room getting in there."

Tobin scampered deeper inside, giving the snake plenty of room to wiggle. Hess wedged his nose into cracks along the floor, using his snout to pull himself up. He flexed his stomach muscles and smoothly slid the rest of the way in.

Tobin scurried ahead around the bend until the passage split in two. "Which way do you suppose they went?"

Hess flicked his tongue. "This way."

The snake pulled ahead, and Tobin trotted behind, admiring Hubbart's handiwork. The woodchuck's den was the most complex piece of tunneling he'd ever seen. Hess's tongue led the way along a shaft that wove and ducked around a massive knot of tree roots. Tobin imagined an enormous tree looming above. The light faded as they plunged deeper into the warren, passing huge, hollowed-out chambers filled with turnips and other delicacies. It was cool and dark, reminding Tobin of home.

Tobin tried peeking around Hess, but it was difficult to gauge his swerve. "Are we getting close to the others?"

"Yes," said Hess, "I smell fresh air."

A moment later the draft hit Tobin's nose. A shaft ahead glowed with sunlight, and Tobin heard the familiar voice of his sister chatting. "Maybe I should head up first, Hess. So Hubbart knows you're—er, *we're* coming."

Hess slid over. "Good idea."

Tobin sprang into the shaft and scrambled up. His nose popped into the open air between two bushy clumps of switchgrass, the long, rough blades providing perfect camouflage.

"Tobin," Talia called. Sitting beneath stems so lengthy they'd stooped over, Talia, Wiley, and Hubbart all looked at him expectantly.

"Guess what?" said Wiley. "Hubbart thinks we're getting close to the Arakni lair."

The good news made Tobin's stomach flip. Joining his friends, he looked up to the woodchuck. "So, they filled you in on our story, huh?"

"Sure did," Hubbart said, just as Hess slithered out from the ground. "The four of ya make a pretty unusual lot."

Tobin remembered a particular possum that would share that sentiment. "Yeah, I suppose we do. Thanks for letting us travel through your burrow, it's pretty amazing."

"Why, thank ya, lad." Hubbart raised his chin, glancing in the direction of the den. "It's been in the family for generations. We just keep expanding."

Talia glanced across the tiny patch of meadow before the forest again grew thick. "Where is your family, Hubbart?"

"Oh, they're down in the 'belly o' the den,' as we call it."

Hess finished rubbing his cheeks on the ground. "Your family has one of the most elaborate dwellings I've ever seen."

"Is that so?" Hubbart raised a furry brow. "I suppose a serpent such as you has been through many, many such dwellings."

Tobin's heart skipped a beat. For the love of wheat, why taunt a *snake*?

The corner of Hess's mouth twitched into a little smile. "I suppose I have. But those would be stories for another day."

Hubbart guffawed, his quake of laughter quivering the grass. Relieved that everyone's senses of humor seemed intact, Tobin exhaled his breath. He had no desire to ever ask Hess about those stories. "We should get moving. Hubbart, you said we're getting close to the Arakni lair?"

"Ah, my little band o' misfits." Hubbart's cheery expression sagged. "Yer almost there."

fifteen

TOBIN GRIMACED AT HUBBART'S words. "Your den is close to the spiders?"

Hubbart's fur bristled. "Rah! Vermin most foul. Once a year, they traipse across this crevice. None too big a concern for me—me an' my kin stomp every arachnid that's stepped a leg in the warren." Hubbart pointed to nearby stone. "That's where we chuck the nasty carcasses, to try 'n' give any trespassing spider fair warning."

Tobin cringed looking at the grotesque cemetery; there had to be a dozen freshly crushed spider husks scattered around the stone.

"Brazen beasties," continued Hubbart. "I'd swear by my third paw those spiders are throwing nature's balance into a tizzy. Yesterday I saw an Arakni try to make off with a wee chick right from a hawk's nest."

Wiley's eyes doubled in size. "Aren't they scared of anything?"

Hubbart shook his head. "Not that I reckon. Mind you—it ain't bravery, Arakni's just not bright enough to *be* scared. I can tell ya, that mama hawk swooped in and squished that spider to bits before it even got into the nest."

Talia shivered. "I'm glad."

"Are ya cheering for a hawk now?" asked Hubbart. His brow furrowed. "Common enemies make for strange friends. Present company included."

Hess slithered past, snaking back toward the crevice they'd just crossed.

Tobin's ears perked. "Where're you going?"

"Just looking for any straggling spiders," Hess called back. "Stay put."

Hubbart shrugged. "Anyway, I think the hunt is over. Dozens of the beasties crawled past yesterday and I ain't seen many since."

Wiley's ears drooped. "Ugh. You saw dozens?"

"Aye. They climb into the gorge from every which direction, but when they climb out"—Hubbart turned his head—"they all head toward that hillside."

Tobin's heart fluttered uncomfortably fast as he forced

himself to follow Hubbart's gaze. Past the little patch of meadow, into the forest, a scattering of pine trees stood higher than the rest. And hidden somewhere on that pine-covered hill, the Arakni lair waited.

"I know yer endeavor is an honorable one, but . . ." Hubbart grimaced. "But I think maybe ya should consider leaving the mouseling here while ya scout things out a bit."

The whites of Talia's eyes flashed as she looked from Tobin to Hubbart. "No. No, I want to stay with my brother."

Tobin met her worried stare. She'd handled herself just fine, better than fine—so far. But things were about to get more dangerous. And it wasn't long ago she was a pinkling herself. What if the Arakni snatched her, too?

Tobin shuddered. "Tal, you were a huge help tracking the spiders, but now, maybe if there's a safe place for you to wait—"

"No!" Instantly, Talia's whiskers drooped. "You can't leave me."

"She's coming with us." Hess slid up behind Hubbart, his golden eyes fixed on the hillside. "And we need to get moving."

Tobin took a step forward. "But she can stay with

Hubbart. She's small, Hess, and where we're going is so dangerous—"

"I heard." Hess turned, staring Tobin dead in the eyes. "But she's right. Her place is with us. So let's move. Now."

Without another word, Hess slithered toward the open meadow. Talia scrambled to Hess's side. "I'm glad at least *you* understand."

Anger threatened to sizzle through Tobin's composure. When did Hess appoint himself boss? "You're just going to make decisions for all of us now?"

"On this matter," Hess called out, then gave a curt nod. "Yes." The snake turned again toward the forest. "Let's move."

Hubbart scratched his chin. "You got a flea for a brain in there, snake?"

Hess disappeared into the deep grass of the meadow, Talia trotting alongside. "We have to go," said Wiley, running after them.

Tobin's eyes burned as he watched his companions slip away. "Unbelievable," he muttered before scurrying after them. Here he'd thought they were a *team*. And then just like that, their journey was now on Hess's terms—and how much could the snake really care about them, if he wouldn't even consider what might be safest for Talia?

Hubbart hollered as Tobin entered the meadow, "Tobin! Yer free to use my tunnels on yer way back if ya need."

Tobin waved his tail, acknowledging Hubbart's offer as he tromped after his friends.

Once he caught up, Wiley leaned close and whispered, "I know you're mad. I don't get it, either. But try and forget about it for now."

Tobin gritted his teeth.

Wiley continued. "Where we're going, you need to have a clear mind."

Tobin snorted. Really? Of *all* mice . . . "Who are you to tell me anything about thinking clearly?"

Flattening his scabbed ear, Wiley froze in his tracks and rounded on him.

Sludge.

"Who am *I?*" Wiley's dark eyes flashed a shade darker. "I'm your friend, turd-for-brains. And I know you're steamed up right now, but believe me, you'll regret doing something dumb . . . like pitching a fit when we should be watching for Arakni."

"I know." Tobin winced. "I'm sorry. I just don't understand what happened back there. Hubbart made a fair point about Talia. Hess just turned all elder-in-charge on us."

Wiley shrugged. "Maybe he did for a second, right back there. But he's actually listened to us—well, you—a lot today."

"He sure didn't listen when I told him Talia should stay at Hubbart's place!"

Wiley shook his head. "I know. Maybe he didn't trust Hubbart. Who knows, but we'd better catch up; they're almost in the woods."

Hess and Talia were waiting for them at the fringe of the forest. Hess's long tongue flashed in and out, collecting odorous information before they entered.

Approaching in silence, Tobin also used his nose. This forest smelled . . . *old*. The aroma of rotting pine needles and moss-covered limbs hung thick in the air. Rising onto his hind legs, Tobin saw the ground ahead was a deep tangle of broken branches and debris. It must have been eons since a fire had cleansed these woods.

Hess cocked his head. "I've heard of this," he said very matter-of-factly. "A section of woodland, protected by barriers, lies undisturbed by flood or fire. In this case, the gorge we crossed and the back side of this hill protect this stretch of forest."

Talia crinkled her nose. "It's awfully musty."

"Yes." Wiley nodded thoughtfully. "It smells like raccoon pee."

Hess nodded. "You're right. There are raccoons in these woods, but they should be sleeping this time of day. Still . . ." Hess looked to Tobin. "I'd suggest you three climb onto my back. It'll be safer. Is that okay with you?"

Now he wants my opinion? Tobin shrugged. "Fine."

Hess swerved his midsection toward the mice. "Climb on."

Talia hopped past Tobin, but before she climbed aboard, she glanced at him. Her eyes were wide, hopeful. Tobin knew she wanted everything to be okay between them. He forced a smile, hoping it would pacify her—despite the sting he still felt.

Talia grinned back, a look of relief spreading across her face. She turned, quickly scaling Hess's side. Tobin sighed quietly as Wiley moved past him. "Atta mouse," Wiley whispered, then he, too, leaped atop the snake's back.

Tobin was about to jump when he saw Hess's eyes cut to him. Tobin stopped, meeting his gaze. Hess swallowed, like the words he wanted to speak were about to choke him. Tobin wanted to know why Hess insisted on Talia coming with them, but he raised his paw to stop the explanation, knowing whatever the serpent was about to say would probably make him mad all over again.

Despite Tobin's protest, Hess inched his head nearer. "I had a good reason. Please believe me. We have to keep moving." Then the snake swiped his head back toward the ancient woods. "Hop on."

Feeling a bit numb, Tobin jumped. The dread of plunging into unknown waters washed over him. Hess was not telling him everything.

As Tobin settled in, Wiley looked at him with a suspicious squint. Wiley probably wanted to know what Hess had said, but Tobin himself wasn't sure what to make of it. So he shrugged, shaking his head and digging his claws into the rubbery snakeskin. Tobin knew the truth was coming.

As Hess slipped forward toward the ancient forest, Tobin drew a deep breath. He couldn't worry about Hess's strangeness now. The ancient forest loomed ahead. The Arakni. Their pinkling.

Everything else must wait.

sixteen

THE JAGGED CAW OF a crow cut the stillness above. Tobin raised his eyes but couldn't see the bird through the matted canopy. The caw was the only noise he'd heard since they'd slipped into this decrepit forest. Decomposers ruled these woods; every wooden surface with inches to spare was sprinkled with lichen and mushrooms. There were no small birds, toads, or even ants to be seen. It was only a matter of time before the larger animals abandoned this wood—if they hadn't already.

"Spider," Wiley whispered.

By now Tobin knew the drill. Hess slid them out of sight, this time behind a mound of tree limbs draped with moss. The cluttered forest provided plenty of hideouts. This was good, since they'd already hidden five times and were only halfway up the hill.

Still perched atop Hess's back, Tobin stood carefully on his hind legs and gazed through a slit in the fuzz-covered branches. An Arakni scurried up the hill; a captive cricket chirped in its sack. A flutter of motion near the base of the hill caught Tobin's eye. Another Arakni started up the hill, but this spider hobbled beneath a strange load. Tobin squinted, then almost chuckled: this Arakni had caught a snail, though it was unclear now who was stuck to whom. The land snail had almost broken free of its webbing and slid onto the side of the spider's rear, looking like a crusty, spiral-shaped growth.

Tobin spoke softly to his companions. "Another spider. This one's a slow mover."

Wiley rolled his eyes. "Then I'm stretching my legs." He hopped off Hess's back and hit the mushy substrate, stretching out one leg and then another.

Tobin glanced again through the crack, shaking his head.

"Lemme see." Talia crept over, nudging her head under his chin. Her eyes crinkled at the sight of the spider-riding snail, and a smile spread across her face.

Tobin watched Wiley sniff the soft ground. Suddenly his friend cocked his head, an ear pivoting downward. "Oh yeah."

Quick as a tail flick, Tobin hopped off Hess and landed squarely beside his friend.

Wiley rubbed his front paws. "Smell anything?"

Tobin sniffed, but Wiley wasn't waiting for his answer—Wiley plunged his paws into the composting ground, wrapped his claws around something, and pulled. "Grab here, c'mon!"

Tobin caught a whiff—worm. A *big* one. The scent woke a hunger pain in his belly. Digging his claws in, Tobin felt the slimy skin and squeezed. Gritty goo squished through his paws as he yanked.

With a hushed voice Talia called down to them. "What are you guys doing?"

"Got a night crawler here," Wiley grunted.

Tobin got both paws around it. "Got it,"

With a final heave, Wiley pulled a section of the night crawler from the ground. Tobin snipped the worm in two with his front teeth, the severed half curling around his paws.

Tobin looked up to Talia. "Want a bite?"

She shook her head. "Yuck. Those taste like wet dirt."

To be polite, Tobin held up a section to Hess, who watched them—as he often did—with his head cocked in curiosity.

161

"No, go ahead," said Hess. "I'll keep watch, you all eat."

Wiley shrugged, shoving a clawful of worm in his mouth. He muttered between lip smacks, "Good . . . protein."

"So is this." Talia hopped off Hess's back and scurried to a patch of grayish lichens blooming like broccoli off a tree root. She swiped a pawful and held it out for them to see. "Reindeer lichen. See? 'Cause if you look close it looks like little crisscrossed antlers."

Tobin nodded. "Someone's paying attention in class."

"But how's it taste?" Wiley asked.

Talia shrugged. "I haven't tried it in a while. Here goes." She stuffed her cheeks and chomped away, her forehead scrunching as she considered the flavor. "Kind of like dandelion root."

"I'll stick with worm," said Wiley, who smiled at Tobin. "You might have a little competition for Top Gatherer when Talia hits junior class."

Talia beamed. Sitting upright, she turned her head in Tobin's direction, waiting for his reply. *Hoping for a pat on the back*, he realized. "What can I say? It must run in the family."

The lichen in her cheeks almost spilled out as she chewed and smiled at the same time. "Hope so! Then I can be a weather scout, too."

"Weather scout?" Hess spoke while keeping his gaze fixed on the woods. "What about your rescue scout idea?"

"Well, that's not really a thing," Talia said.

"Maybe not yet," Hess replied.

Tobin wiped the last trace of crawler off his face. "I suppose this is as good a time as any to talk about a plan."

Wiley spoke, wiping the last of worm goo from his snout. "You have anything in mind?"

"Nothing *too* specific," Tobin said, "but I've been adding up what we know about the Arakni, and I think we have something in common with them."

"Eww," Talia said. "Don't say that."

"Well, it's true. We both gather food and then store it. Like the bee colonies Camrik talked about."

"You think they stash those websacks together somewhere?" Wiley asked.

"It could be." Hess nodded. "I suppose an arachnid colony could store food in a central location. Except . . ." Hess abruptly looked away, like his mind needed a little space.

"They remind me of something else, too. Like a pack—a wolf pack, returning spoils to the den," Hess said.

Wiley stepped forward. "But so far, the pinkling,

the cricket—they keep their captives alive. Wolves . . ." Wiley shivered. "Wolves don't."

"I can't figure that out." Hess shook his head, adding grimly, "I suppose we'll learn soon enough."

Nervousness fluttered in Tobin's stomach. "Maybe we should talk about scouting ahead. It would help if we can find their food storage."

Wiley raised his head. "Well, I volunteer for that. These treetops are woven so tight, I figure I can climb up one trunk and then hop the canopy tops until I see the lair."

"I'll go with you," Tobin said. "Four eyes are better than two."

Talia's ears perked. "Me too?"

Tobin shook his head. "You wait with Hess this time. We'll be sprinting full-speed for this trip." Tobin looked to Hess. "Agreed?"

"Agreed," Hess said; his huge sides caved in and out as he sighed. "Though I hate splitting up, we do need to play to our strengths. Watch for returning Arakni. Move quick. Be safe."

Tobin knew scouting was risky, but staying behind was dreadful. He nudged Talia with his tail. "We'll be fast—and careful."

Wiley nodded, adding, "Just another year, Tal, and you'll be able to keep up on a scouting run, no problem."

She nodded with a gulp.

Glancing at Wiley, Tobin hopped to an open crevice in the moss-covered branches. Wiley followed and crouched next to him. Together they stared at the unfamiliar woods ahead.

Wiley stretched his hind legs. "You ready for this?"

Over his shoulder, Tobin caught sight of Talia hopping onto Hess's back, settling in behind his head. "I guess so."

Wiley scratched his chin. "I can't think of a Rule advising using a snake as a mouseling sitter."

For a moment Tobin almost laughed, but his throat was too dried out from nerves. "There aren't any Rules for this." Tobin narrowed his focus on the closest tree. "I think we're making up our own rules now."

seventeen

A SCOUTING JOB. TOBIN just needed to think of it as an everyday scouting trip. Shouldn't be too difficult. Same technique as seeking food, just tweaked accordingly. Instead of scouting for seeds, scout for information. Tobin would choose the path, Wiley would follow. Same as always, right?

Deep breath, clear your mind.

Select destination. Tree, one hare-leap away.

Scan for hawks. Done. Tree canopies eerily still, in fact.

Seek possible threats from ground predators. Done. No movement, no smells, no sounds.

Select route least likely for ambush. Done.

Go.

Tobin darted, his paws hitting the ground with precision. It took six heartbeats to reach the tree. Never slowing, he leaped, his claws digging into the bark. He spiraled up the trunk so they wouldn't be easy pickings. Not until he reached the thick cover of canopy did Tobin reduce his pace, opting for the shelter of an abandoned squirrel nest. He wriggled into a space between the hunk of mud and leaves, sitting only a few heartbeats until Wiley squirmed in beside him.

They sat in silence, waiting to see if their jaunt attracted any attention. A wisp of a breeze rustled the highest tree limbs, but below, the forest sat in stillness.

Tobin nodded to Wiley. He crept from the shelter of the nest, studying the crisscrossing limbs ahead. He needed his bearing on the direction of the Arakni lair. He looked down.

For the love of wheat, they were up high. Way, *way* high. Even a full-grown buck couldn't swipe his antlers and knock these boughs. Sure, he'd been in trees before, but maybe those were saplings? His mind felt a little swimmy, so he gripped the bark harder. *Oh, sludge.* Tobin shut his eyes and concentrated. What's the Rule?

Rule #16: Mice are not arboreal and belong near the ground. (If you somehow find yourself in a tree, see Rule #17.)

Ah, that's right. So . . .

*Rule #17: If you climb too high—take a deep breath,
imagine an acorn at your end destination, and never,
EVER, look down.*

Tobin's eyes popped open. *An acorn?* Well, it was worth a try. Deep breath. Eyes ahead.

Picture the nut.

He spied a good spot to imagine an acorn—right in the neighboring tree, at the base of a very stable-looking branch. It was only about two hare-leaps . . . *leaps?* No—no thinking about *leaps* right now, think *scoots.* Like an inchworm. Focus on an imaginary acorn about a hundred inchworm-scoots away.

Tobin scooted. Left paw, right paw, hind paws. The bough felt solid beneath him, so he inched faster. He knew he probably looked ridiculous, like a skulking bobcat, but he did not care. Wiley could tease him all he wanted when they got *down on the ground.*

Crawling to an intersection where the long branches of two neighboring trees crisscrossed, Tobin climbed onto the new tree. He scurried inward until he reached the trunk, right where he'd pictured the imaginary acorn.

"Well," said Wiley, sidling up alongside him. "We're getting close. Look."

Following Wiley's sight line, Tobin looked down.

Beneath them on the forest floor, two hunting spiders scuttled toward the lair. The spiders' path was clear. There, about a dozen trees over, a boulder-sized mound of mud and forest debris rose from ground, and the Arakni swarmed around it. The sight sent a quiver down Tobin's spine, and he clenched the bark as hard as he could.

Wiley leaned in beside him. "We need to get a few more trees over. Then we'll have a real birds-eye view of the layout."

Tobin nodded and swallowed.

Wiley cocked an ear. "You okay?"

Tobin pursed his mouth shut before turning away from Wiley's suspicious stare. "Yeah, I'm just getting used to the heights." He drew a deep breath, then shook his head. "All right, let's check for hawks and get moving."

He tilted his head, looking for birds of prey, when his eyes fell upon a glossy, golden streak of liquid on the trunk, just above his head. "Wait a sec." Tobin raised onto his hind legs. Squinting, he reached a paw up and touched the trickle.

Sap.

Usually he hated the stuff; a glob of sap could stick in your fur until the springtime shed if a mouse wasn't careful. But now it could be just the thing to make this tree-traversing much safer. "Check this out." Tobin smeared the sap on one paw, then the other. "Sticky paws, a tree-climbing mouse's best friend."

A smile crept across Wiley face. "Nice!" Wiley dabbed his paws in the gummy goop and clapped them together. He tried pulling them apart, and his brow furrowed when it actually took some effort.

Tobin flexed his toes, the clingy, sticky stuff pulling on his paw pads. "Maybe this is how squirrels don't fall."

"Could be." Wiley kneaded the bark beneath him, the *snick-snick* of sticky sap sounding very reassuring.

Tobin examined the crossroad of trees and branches ahead. One prickly pine a few trees over would give them a perfect spot for spying on Arakni. "There." He pointed, showing the tree to Wiley. Tobin scurried out onto the woven canopy branches, making sure to never look down. With his gummy grip it felt safer to move faster, crossing from tree to tree, until they reached the final pine. After wedging himself against the brittle tree trunk, Tobin finally allowed himself to look down.

He winced. "It's sort of like looking down at an ant mound, only replace the ants—"

"with giant spiders," Wiley completed his thought.

Tobin spied one lower, slender limb that stretched

out over all the Arakni activity, including the far side of the mound. "Wait here," he said to Wiley, then pointed down. "I'm gonna climb out on that branch, but it gets pretty narrow. No sense putting two of us on it."

Wiley frowned, slowly shaking his head. "I don't know, Tobin."

"We need to know what's on the other side of that mound, and that's the only branch that reaches all the way over."

"Well,"—Wiley ran a sticky paw over his nose, his nerves quite apparent—"I suppose you do have that inchworm technique down pretty well."

Tobin smiled in reply and then shimmied down the trunk of the pine. Flattening himself to the wispy branch, he crept out until the warm, thick stink of the spiders assaulted his nose. Stretching out his neck, Tobin peeked over the side for a perfect bird's-eye view.

A rotting tree stump sat tilted on the ground, partially pulled from the earth. Ripped-up roots spilled over an open cavity beneath it. The few shards of light that pierced the black space revealed mottled shadows of scuttling legs and the occasional glint of red eyes. A spider stepped from the cavern, emerging with a small stone clutched in its rear pincers. Like it was excavating the cavern. Smaller than the hunting Arakni he'd seen, but thicker than the scouting Arakni, Tobin realized this must be a worker.

The ground seemingly belched these smaller worker spiders, one by one, from the holes around their home. They discarded their loads on the surface before retreating back into the darkness.

So, if these were the worker Arakni, where were . . .

There. Tobin's muscles clenched at the sight of it, a hunter returning. This Arakni was huge. As long as a robin. The worker spiders looked like hummingbirds compared to their predatory siblings. The hunter stomped past the work site to a dilapidated tree trunk. Probably the tree that had broken off the stump. Tobin raised his chin and watched the hunter slip through a gash in the fallen log, its pulsing websack in tow. Tobin held his breath, not wanting to move or even blink. A few heartbeats later, the Arakni reemerged, pincers empty.

The food storage. That's where all the captives were taken. And that's where he'd find his little sibling.

Time to get back to Hess, to Talia. They needed to find a way to this log. Maybe they could wind around the back of the hill. But first he and Wiley needed to get down off these trees.

Tobin inched back along the branch and scaled up the trunk to where he'd left Wiley. At least, where he thought he left Wiley. He looked left, right—then noticed something that hadn't been there before.

His heart pounded against his breastbone. A white smear dotted the branch. A goopy and unmistakably acidic-smelling blob.

Owl poop.

eighteen

QUICK AS A FLICK, Tobin skittered to the underside
of the branch, claws clenching the bark as he hung upside
down. His throat tightened.

What have I done?

Bringing his friend to this terrible place? His sister?
His head mimicked a bobbing leaf as he looked for any
sign of Wiley. Or the owl. But the only movement came
from the Arakni below. Tobin shivered. *Hopefully spiders
don't look up often.*

He let go of the branch, tucked into a flip, and landed
on the limb below. He wedged himself under a piece of
curled bark.

Breathe. Think.

Fresh owl poop in the middle of the day? Also, he'd
been the one sitting totally out in the open whenever this

owl flew by. Why hadn't it grabbed him?

Things weren't adding up.

Tchirr, tchirr, tchirr!

Hope swelled in his chest as the sounds filled his ears. Swiveling his head, a movement caught his eye; there, one tree over, a familiar tail waved from behind a cluster of three pine cones.

Tobin let go a relieved puff of breath as he zeroed in on the pine-cone cluster. Trusting Wiley wouldn't call him over unless it was safe, Tobin bolted. He skimmed the length of branch and hopped onto his friend's bough. Darting behind the pine cones, he saw Wiley's eyes were as wide as acorn caps.

Wiley held up his paw, spreading two toes. "We were *this close* to becoming tomorrow's owl pellets."

Tobin shook his head. "What happened?"

Wiley shrugged. "I can't explain it. I heard the swish of feathers and thought I was done for. I looked up and saw a real cranky-looking hooter sitting one branch up from me. Thing is, I know that owl saw me. And you, too. But it just watched you, like it wondered what you were looking at." Wiley scowled. "Then that lice bag tried to poop on me. And away it flew."

Tobin cringed—good grief, how'd he not noticed an

owl breathing down his back? "Maybe it's sick? Something's got to be wrong with an owl that's out during the day."

"I don't know, but we should get back to Talia and Hess. Let 'em know we have an owl to worry about now, too."

Just great. Another oddity to add to the list. Tobin nodded, and they ran across the canopy. Though the stickiness on his paws was nearly gone, the added fear of a nearby owl was motivation enough to haul tail.

The musty scent of the forest floor welcomed Tobin as he spiraled down the final tree, away from the Arakni lair and back into Talia and Hess's hideout. He barely scurried through the moss-covered entrance when Talia pounced. "You're back!" She threw her paws around his neck, knocking him a step back.

"It was quite a trip." Tobin shifted his gaze to Hess. "And a successful one. We saw the lair and the food storage."

Wiley leaped past him, landing squarely between Talia and Hess. "And we saw an owl! Actually, it saw us first, but it didn't even try to eat us."

Hess's tail curled around a nearby stick. "An owl?" He looked up, peering through the tiny holes in their hideout as if they were gaping crags. His head swiveled. "What did this owl look like?"

What does that matter? Tobin shook his head. "Wiley's the only one who saw it."

Wiley's ears flicked back with excitement. "It was huge! Brown feathers tipped with black, and its beak was jagged. I think there was a chip on the side of it. And it looked cranky."

Hess lowered his head, sucking in a deep breath. "I think I know this owl."

The tone of Hess's voice made the skin on Tobin's paws prickle. "You *know* this owl? What do you mean?" Dread welled in his stomach like dirty water.

"His name is Swallfyce. He occasionally works with my mother."

Wiley tapped his chin. "Wait a sec, did you say an owl works with your mom?"

"It's a very new arrangement," said Hess. "My mother's worry over the recent Arakni population explosion has become an obsession. It's led to some interesting partnerships. Us included, I suppose."

Tobin went cold. Hess had secrets. Secrets with dangerous implications. "What does your mother have to do with this?"

"Remember the snake queen you met, Queen Hesthpa?"

The mice nodded.

Hess sighed. "She is my mother."

Wiley sat upright. "That gigantic snake is your *mom*?"

Hess nodded. "Yes."

Talia grabbed her tail, stroking it through her paws. Her nose scrunched. "She said you were just her interpreter, not her son."

"My mother often speaks in half-truths. I *am* her interpreter," said Hess, "but I also hatched from her brood. So many of us call her 'mother' that the title seems inconsequential."

Tobin tapped a claw on the ground, trying to jog his memory of that very first meeting with the snakes. "What'd your mother whisper to you right before we left?"

Hess pursed his scale-ridged lips together as he thought. "My mother said, 'Mice are clever. Help them find the lair and a way the snakes can travel there. Learn all you can.'"

Tobin's whiskers twitched, and Hess sighed. "I swear, Tobin. I didn't think she'd follow us with an army."

"Huh?" Tobin leaned in toward Hess. "What do you mean, follow us with an army?"

Hess stared off in the distance, solving a riddle only

he had the clues to. "I think that was her plan all along. She used me—well, us actually—to find a way across that gorge."

Wiley ears flattened. "Why?"

"The Arakni raided her most recent clutch of eggs, snatching a few hatchlings just as they broke from the shell. My mother was . . . enraged, to say the least. She says the spiders have grown too aggressive."

"So what does a cranky owl have to do with the spiders?" asked Talia.

Hess looked skyward. "If Swallfyce is here, I'd say she's recruited a parliament of owls to help."

"Why owls?" Talia asked. "Why would they fight for her?"

"Fight *with* her. Yes, the Arakni are catching the occasional hatchlings, and that angers the queen. But that is hardly the spiders' biggest violation. No, the Arakni are overhunting everything. The forest is falling out of balance. If the Arakni population continues to spread, all of the forest will look as dismal as this decrepit stretch." Hess paused before thinking out loud. "Yes, I believe my mother teamed up with owls to destroy the Arakni lair."

Tobin began kneading the dirt beneath his paws. This

changed everything. *Everything!* "What about our pinkling?" he asked. "When will this spider-attacking army get here? We need to rescue our pinkling before they come!"

Hess frowned. "I don't know, Tobin. I'm sorry. I think the most prudent plan would be to continue our own mission."

"How?" Tobin flung the dirt in his paws against the log shelter. "The proof is the poop! The owls are here. And the snakes—they must be right on our tails."

"Spiders, snakes, *and* owls?" Talia shivered. "Oh, sludge."

Wiley's whiskers suddenly twitched like he'd been stung by a deerfly. "Wait, wouldn't that mean—if the snakes are following us—won't that lead them to Hubbart's den?"

Tobin's throat went as dry as sunbaked tree bark. Hess had acted strangely right after they left Hubbart's den, right after he'd looked into the gorge. Tobin had been too upset with him about risking Talia when it happened to think any more of it, but now— "Through," he corrected. "*Through* Hubbart's den."

Hess nodded slowly, his tongue flicking in and out. "The snakes have already been through Hubbart's."

Talia raised her chin. "How would you know that, Hess?"

Hess's tail squeezed the stick until it cracked. "When we left Hubbart's den, I saw them."

"Saw who?" Tobin asked, even though he already knew the answer. The growl in his voice surprised him.

Hess's reptilian eyes met Tobin's. "Snakes. Dozens of snakes, descending into the gorge and heading toward Hubbart's den."

"Why didn't you say anything?" Talia cried.

"Because I needed to get you three away from there!" Hess snapped.

Tobin heard Wiley drawing shaky breaths. His friend's ears and nose were flushed.

"But Hubbart helped us," Wiley whispered. "He helped us, and we brought him nothing but a snake army."

Hess sucked in a sharp breath. "Had I known my mother's plan, I'd have told Hubbart to join his family deep in the den and hide." Hess looked intently at each mouse. "But I didn't know the plan."

"We still could have warned him," Wiley shouted.

"You wouldn't have left Hubbart's den had I told you," Hess replied. "You weren't safe with the snake army coming."

Tobin's heart sank. "Your mother's not the only master of half-truths in the family."

Hess shook his head. "Please understand. Once you discovered a path for the snakes to cross the gorge, in their eyes, you served your purpose. I think that was my mother's plan the whole time. Who knows what they would have done to you. Anyway, Hubbart already said his family was 'down in the belly o' the den.'" Hess cleared his throat. "Hubbart's a big woodchuck. I'm sure he handled himself well."

"That's why!" said Talia, her eyes flashed with understanding. "That's why you said I couldn't stay at Hubbart's. Tobin wanted me to wait with Hubbart, but you said no. You said my place was with you."

"Yes." Hess nodded. "You might not believe it, but I only wanted to keep you safe. And what's more, I have an assignment. I was—*am*—to escort you three to find the Arakni lair. What other schemes my mother may hatch in the forest are not my concern."

Talia gripped her tail again. "You mean, you still plan on helping us?"

"All the way," Hess answered, then looked to Tobin, waiting for his response.

About a dozen questions and accusations bounced around Tobin's brain, but one seemed particularly important. "What happens when your mother shows up?"

"Yeah." Wiley nodded. "If your mom comes along and decides we should be snake chow, will you turn us over?"

Hess flinched. "I can't believe you'd ask that."

Talia stared at him, unrelenting. "Why are you still here?"

Hess tilted his head. "When we began our journey, it was because my mother ordered it. But now I'm here because I know you need my help. And I *want* to give it. I admire what you're doing, and I want you to succeed. I want to find the pinkling and bring it home."

Tobin sat back, his left hind leg tapping. Hess left Hubbart to deal with the snakes. Hess didn't tell them they were being followed. Hess wasn't acting like a real teammate; but, it's not exactly like they were at home playing capture-the-berry.

Tobin exhaled sharply. He had one last question for Hess. "Why didn't your mom just ask the owls to carry the snakes across the gorge?"

"It's too dangerous for the snakes," Hess said matter-of-factly. "The risks of puncture wounds from talons, injury upon landing—or dropping—all combined with asking each snake to trust that its owl courier won't decide to just make a meal of its passenger, no, it's too much."

Tobin nodded, letting this last bit of info swirl around in his brain. Was Hess a friend or a swindler?

Honestly, it didn't matter. Not at this point. Tobin cleared his throat. "We can sort all this 'who knew what' out later. In front of us is the Arakni colony. Behind us, an army of predators is coming for the spiders. We need to keep moving, and we need to save our pinkling."

Wiley scratched his head. "So, when the snakes and owls show up, we just hope no one tries to make a meal out of us?"

"I should think that when the snakes and owls storm the Arakni lair, they'll be rather busy," answered Hess.

Sure, Tobin thought. *They won't give much thought to a snake slithering off with three mice and a pinkling riding on its back.*

Talia folded her paws across her chest. "But what if they decide they aren't too busy for a quick bite?"

A menacing look flickered across Hess's gold eyes. "I'll encourage them to reconsider."

nineteen

TOBIN'S NOSE TWITCHED AS Talia peered outside their hiding place. Her ears pricked high as she sniffed for any signs of trouble. After what seemed like enough time to chew through five walnuts, she finally ducked back in. "Good news: I think most of the spiders must have returned to the lair. I've only seen one scuttle past."

"That is good news," Wiley said.

"Yeah." Talia scratched her cheek. "But, here's the bad news. There is definitely a big brown owl with a cranky face in a pine tree staring at us. Is that Swallfyce?"

"Ugh." Tobin swiped at the dirt with his paw. "Hess, we don't have time for this."

Hess raised his head, his lip curling.

"Let me see what the old crank has to say." Hess slithered from their shelter.

The owl's head bobbed to the side as it watched Hess slither into the open. Hess raised his head, calling to the big bird. "Come on down," he said, adding more quietly, "you cantankerous coot."

Swallfyce jumped off his perch and swooped down, his wing-flapping landing procedure sending a cloud of dust in the direction of Tobin and his crew.

Hess coughed then shook the dust off his snout. "Hello, Swallfyce. It's been a while."

"I'd say." The owl's voice was a strange mixture of squawky and gravelly, and he regarded Hess with his giant yellow eyes. "You were no more than an oversize night crawler last I saw you."

Hess smirked at the comment. "I don't know about that."

Swallfyce cocked his large head to the side, his ear feathers nearly touching his shoulder. "So, what are you still doing here, boy?"

"Boy?" Hess straightened back up.

"Shouldn't you be heading back to meet yer mother? You found the location of the spider lair." Swallfyce snapped his head back up and glared at Hess. The big owl puffed out his feathers, transforming into quite an imposing figure.

"That wasn't the deal." Talia jumped from the shelter

186

and stepped forward; Hess immediately swerved between her and the owl.

"And who are you?" Swallfyce bent forward, almost comically low. Tobin couldn't help but feel like something was off about this owl.

"I'm Talia, and Queen Hesthpa herself ordered Hess to be our escort, and we still need him."

"Is that right?" Swallfyce chuckled, then began to pace back and forth, keeping his stare on Talia, his head pivoting with each step.

"I'm accompanying the mice, Swallfyce. I'm sure you, my mother, the whole army—have things well under control."

"There's the problem." The owl pointed his wing feathers directly at Hess. "You, boy. She wants you to turn around and rejoin the snakes. I think it's rubbing her scales the wrong way not having you on the front line with her. So head on back down this hill a ways and check in. Maybe she'll even let you rejoin your little posse here."

Hess snorted. "We both know that won't happen. She doesn't need me. These mice, they do. They fulfilled what my mother wanted of them—they found a route for the snakes to cross the gorge. So, I'll stay and help them."

Swallfyce's cheeks puffed up, almost looking like the

owl was snickering. "Then allow me to relay your mother's command." The owl cleared his throat and recited his memorized message: "Dear Son, if you want to remain one of my Favored Children, you will return and fight this battle by my side. If you abandon me now, know that your status will be stripped from you upon your disgraceful return home."

When he finished his message, Swallfyce narrowed his eyes, glaring at Hess. "So, *favored child*, what will you do?"

Hess's upper lip raised, showing his sharp bone-white teeth. "Leave, Swallfyce. Now."

Though Hess spoke evenly, Tobin heard a strain in his voice and thought the snake might have actually shaken with anger.

"Fool." Swallfyce shook his head. "All for what? Dinner?"

Swallfyce lunged, and Hess slid in front of the mice.

He hissed, a low, terrible rumble. "I'll snap your ancient bones like dead twigs, you old lice bag."

Swallfyce froze, then began to shake. Then began to laugh. "Ah, you unpredictable serpents." The owl stretched his wings, preparing to depart. "You know, this is a more entertaining outcome for me anyway. I can't

188

wait to see the look on your mother's face." The owl's voice dripped with disdain. "Farewell, former favorite."

Swallfyce leaped into the air, flapping his sizable wings, leaving them in the dust. The four sat in silence for a few moments, the enormity of the conversation weighing on them.

"Hess, I'm sorry," Wiley finally said. "I believe your mother used you, too, not just us."

"Me too," Tobin agreed. "You're giving up an awful lot to help us."

"You three are the ones risking everything to be here," Hess said softly. "Besides, being a Favored Child is not all it's cracked up to be."

"I'm sure your mother doesn't even mean all that," Talia said, patting Hess on the side.

Hess drew a deep breath. "I'll find out soon enough, I suppose. Now, there's a pinkling who needs us. Immediately, if Swallfyce was right and the snakes are converging just down the hill."

"Then it's time to check out the Arakni's food storage," said Tobin.

"I can carry you over," said Hess. "If you're on my back, I know you're safe. Tobin, you had a good look at the layout. You can direct me where to go."

Three pairs of eyes veered in his direction.

This was it. The last push.

Tobin shifted on his paws. Uncomfortable waves of nerves swirled through his insides, ebbing and flowing all at once. If this rescue mission fell apart, Hess could always carry Talia away from this place.

Tobin nodded. "Before we go, let's agree that if it gets too dangerous out there, we run." He looked to Hess. "The Arakni are storing all those websacks in a rotted-out tree trunk on the back of the hilltop. If Wiley and I get inside that tree trunk and you and Talia get in trouble, get away. We can all meet up at the ridge near Hubbart's. Sound good?"

Talia's face scrunched with despair, the fur on her forehead crinkling. "Why can't I come along and help inside the log?"

Tobin took steadying breaths, trying to say the right words without thinking too much about their meaning and the place he was going. "Because only mice who are big enough to carry a pinkling out of the log need to risk going inside the log."

Talia scowled. "I *am* big enough."

"Another thought I had," Hess interrupted. "We may have the element of surprise on our side. We may be the first to ever try taking anything back from the Arakni, so hopefully there are no guards to watch out for."

Wiley nodded in agreement. "All the more reason to hurry, before the snakes and owls get the spiders on full alert."

"Right." Tobin climbed onto Hess's back, sitting behind the snake's head. He supposed that's where Hess's inner ear was, because of how the snake sometimes tilted his head to listen, and Tobin planned on whispering his directions.

Once all three mice perched aboard, Tobin gave his first direction. "Slide left out of here. The back side of the hill has a steep drop-off. I didn't see any Arakni activity back there. If we can climb it, we can get ourselves closer."

Hess cocked his head slightly, and Tobin guessed the concern. "Don't worry, Hess. It's not as steep as Hubbart's gorge."

Reassured, Hess nodded. "All right, let's move."

After a quick check for spiders, owls, snakes—or anything else that could cause a problem—they slithered out.

The reek became as much a foe as the Arakni themselves; it burned their eyes and clogged their throats. The mice buried their noses into the crooks of their elbows, but Tobin saw Hess's tongue still dutifully flicking, detecting. He couldn't imagine the odorous assault on the snake's senses, and it wasn't until Tobin felt Hess's back muscles quiver beneath him that he knew it was affecting the serpent. Mercifully, the ridge finally curved around to the far side of the hill, and the breeze lessened the stench of the spiders' lair.

Tobin blinked in surprise as he glanced around the landscape; looking from below, not above, offered a *much* different perspective. The back of the hillside was steep, and the reason was clear—a giant boulder rested at the base of the hill. Tobin could see where the dislodged boulder left an open wound near the top of the hillside. Nature tried to patch it, sending running clumps of mud and dustings of debris into the gaping hollow, but it was clear where the boulder had been.

"I can skirt around the indent and make it up." Hess answered the question Tobin had been thinking.

"Sounds good," Tobin said, sliding off Hess's back. "Probably easier if we all climb on our own."

Talia and Wiley nodded, hopping down.

Tobin ran up beside the boulder and waved for them to follow. Once he felt them fall in line behind him, he crept ahead. He spied a route up that Hess should have no trouble following. He glanced right, inched forward, glanced left, and then froze. Except for his eyes. He couldn't open them wide enough.

Between the boulder and the hill sat a pile. A horrid, twisted pile of body parts. It took a few heartbeats for Tobin's brain to place the parts. Arakni parts. Corpses. Some broken, most hollowed out into a husk of the former spider. Crisp exoskeletons, waiting for nature to wear them down to dust.

Knowing he was rattled, Tobin took a step back. Immediately he felt his companions tense, shifting and pressing against the boulder.

He turned to face them. "The dead ones," Tobin croaked, realizing his throat was totally dry. He tried swallowing what little moisture was in his mouth.

"The what?" Wiley whispered.

Attempting another swallow, Tobin tried again. "There's a groove, in the ground right in front of the boulder, about two hare-leaps long." Tobin paused, forcing the shakiness from his voice. "And it is full of dead Arakni. And pieces of dead Arakni."

"Ah, a purging pit." Hess spoke as if he'd seen a hundred of these.

Talia looked at Hess, her nose wriggling in disgust. "Purging pit?"

"It's fairly common among arthropods." Hess looked between them, like he was waiting for this fun fact to register. "Like den cleaning. But for bugs."

"Okay." Wiley nodded, his brows furrowed. "We don't just chuck our deceased in a pit out back, but I get what you're saying."

Tobin shimmied as a chill ran down his spine. "Yuck. So now we all know what to expect, right? Brace yourselves, stay focused on the path."

With that, Tobin turned and faced the steep hillside. *Up and over. Ignore the pit.*

He chose three points of cover; a shrub, a pile of ground vines, and finally, a log resting on the hilltop.

He ran. Sprinting up to the shrub, he heard his companions behind him. Tobin paused, briefly, just enough to check their surroundings. *All clear.* He burst again, darting to the ground vines and plunging between the tangles, feeling the vibrations of his friends joining him. Just as he prepped for their last burst, a scraping, scuttling sound came from above. Tobin flicked his tail. *Freeze!*

They sat as still as stones. Tobin dared to glance upward, wondering what was happening over the ridge. He didn't have to wait long.

Like a squirrel might toss an empty nutshell, two smaller worker Arakni pitched the large body of a hunting Arakni over the ledge. Tobin couldn't help but watch as it soared for a moment, before quite unceremoniously landing in the rotting pile of its brethren. Tobin's ear twitched: Did Wiley just gag?

Not that it mattered, it's not as if any of the spiders on this hillside could harm them. Tobin looked at the pile of corpses one last time, and a horribly disgusting idea popped into his head.

He turned back to his crew. "I know how we can sneak into the food log."

Talia turned her head, eyes peering suspiciously at Tobin. "I'm not sure I'm going to like any ideas inspired by this place."

"Probably not," Tobin admitted. Then he looked toward Hess. "You see any worker spiders in that pile? Preferably two that have been there for a while? You know—just the shell? No gooey bits still stuck inside."

"Ahh." Comprehension filled Hess's voice. "Stay here."

"Oh, Tobin," said Wiley. "No way. Just, no." Wiley's jaw dropped, and he gagged at the thought.

Tobin placed a steadying paw on Wiley's shoulder. "It's just a shell, Wiley. If Hess can find a pair of worker exoskeletons for us, we'll be able to slip right into that food log."

Talia nodded grimly. "It would be the perfect disguise."

Wiley looked helplessly from Talia to Tobin. "Sludge. Of course it's a good idea, it's just also a nasty, terrible, disgusting idea. And I'm usually all for those, but this? Ugh."

"I know, you'll feel better when we get off this hill," said Tobin. "And look, here comes Hess—oh." Tobin cringed. "He's actually carrying the exoskeletons in his mouth, so I think he got the worst of this."

All the color drained from Wiley's ears as he turned to see the awful sight. The remains of two worker spiders, pinched in Hess's mouth, their legs swaying back and forth with the snake's movement.

Hess set the two spider shells down beside them, spitting out the taste before speaking. "These were the best available. They're both missing a leg here and there, but the size is right. Slip under these and you should be able to scurry right in and out."

"Thanks, Hess." Tobin said. "I know this isn't very pleasant."

"We're all in this together, right?" said Hess. "I think these exoskeletons might crumble apart if you try climbing up in them, so I'll carry them up to the ridge. Then you can slip them on."

The mice followed Hess to the log at the top of the hill. From there, Hess slid them into a tangle of ferns, about two hare-leaps down from the toppled tree. "Wait here, I'll take a closer look." Hess spoke the words so softly the vocal vibration tickled Tobin's ears. The snake set the exoskeletons down before slithering halfway to the hollowed-out tree trunk.

Tobin looked to Wiley, whose ears were pricked high and cupped forward. Talia's nose crinkled with concern. Motion caught his eye as Hess rejoined them in the thicket.

"Did you see many spiders?" Tobin asked.

Hess shook his head. "Not many. They appear to enter the log at one end, near the base of the tree. The spiders enter and exit from that opening. And I only saw one straggler." Hess jerked his chin toward the crest of the hill. "Once the hunter spiders deposit their prey, they head back to the main lair. I believe that's what you saw from up in the tree."

"Then we have a chance," Wiley noted.

Tobin looked at Wiley, and his eyes lingered for a moment. Not used to seeing such a serious expression on his friend, he knew they were embarking on something far more daring than stealing an acorn from a blue jay, or pulling a prank on his brother. No, this next stunt had greater stakes than any they'd ever tried before.

Tobin leaned in close to his friend. "I can't imagine going in there with anyone else."

A hint of a smile played on Wiley's muzzle, his whiskers curling just a touch. "Yeah, well, it's nice to know all those years of sneaking into places just may come in handy."

"And we'll keep a close lookout," Talia said, scrambling atop Hess's head. She flattened herself to the back of the snake's skull, her chin resting on the crown of his head, making Hess look like he'd sprouted a second set of tiny brown eyes. Tobin nodded. Talia was in the safest spot around.

"See you both soon." Tobin turned and took a steadying breath. "Here we go." He slipped his nose beneath an exoskeleton, and with a flick of his head created enough space to wriggle beneath the dried-out husk. The carcass scratched against his back, but it was lighter than he anticipated. Tobin wriggled his shoulders until the skeleton was arranged perfectly, draped over his body and sitting just atop his head enough that he could peek out from beneath.

He looked to Wiley, who'd also slid into his disguise.

"This isn't *as* horrible as I thought it'd be," Wiley said.

Tobin gave a quick nod. Nerves were beginning to

fizz in his stomach, and he needed to be calm.

He needed a Rule. He took a steadying breath and looked at the path ahead.

Rule #3: When exploring new terrain—walk softly and keep to the shadows.

Right. It was time.

He crouched low, letting the bony spider legs drag on the ground, and saw Wiley do the same. Tobin nodded to Wiley and slunk away from the ferns, adding a little bounce to his step so the Arakni legs could jostle and shake, like a scuttle. He skirted toward a crabgrass patch sprouting just outside the tunnel entrance. He could hear Wiley scuttle up next to him, and then he heard something else.

He looked up to see a hunter spider exit the log, its long legs scraping the pebbly ground as it crawled up.

Tobin's first instinct was to freeze, but no—if they looked dead, the hunter just might try to pitch them over the ledge, back in the pile.

Tobin turned to face the Wiley-spider. He jerked his body left and right, trying to recreate the Arakni gestures they'd seen along the way. Wiley caught on, and rocked his spider shell back and forth and up and down.

Tobin dared a glance over to the hunter. The spider had paused only a frog-leap away and regarded them for a moment. With a great heave of his shoulder, Tobin attempted to flop a front leg on top of Wiley's shell, like the spider inspections he'd seen them perform earlier. Hopefully, worker spiders performed this ritual, too. The appendage landed, briefly, before sliding off most ungracefully.

Wiley stopped his bouncing and breathed a great sigh. "It turned, Tobin, it's leaving."

Tobin spun around quickly, spider legs flailing around him like a veil of dried twigs. This danger had passed, but there was more to come. It was time to enter the log.

Think of the pinkling.

Think of Mom.

Tobin took a shaky step forward.

He could feel Wiley tensing next to him.

Go.

Tobin marched ahead, forcing himself to be confident in his spider-skin camouflage. In just a few steps they'd reached the opening of the toppled tree trunk, and they peered down into the long, rotted tunnel it had become.

Tobin blinked, trying to get his eyes fine-tuned to the dimness, as his ears picked up the sounds of the captured that floated toward him. Chirps. Buzzes. Squeaks. Soft hisses. If despair had a smell, this place was filthy with it. Mildew and animal waste permeated the sodden bark shell, and Tobin choked on the odor.

When his eyes adjusted, visions, like they were pulled from his own nightmares, hit him from every angle. The whole interior of the log *squirmed*. Websacks lined the inside of the tree husk from ground to ceiling, their captives writhing in misery. The floor was a mush of droppings, insect secretions, and animal parts—tiny jawbones, cricket legs, and even a beak. There was no place to look without observing a new horror, so Tobin turned his head and stared at Wiley. Wiley stared back.

"Cripes, Tobin," Wiley whispered.

The Arakni odor outside seemed mild after exposing his nose to the log filth. "Did you see any spiders in there?"

Wiley shook his head. "Nope. No Arakni, anyway. But I might have seen a wolf spider wrapped up in a websack."

"Cannibals, too, huh? Not really surprised." Tobin shuddered, and he lifted his nose, longing for a breath of the clean air that washed through the treetops above. "Let's get this over with."

Glad to be done with the exoskeleton, Tobin slipped out from beneath the cover of the disguise, and Wiley followed suit, letting the husks drop to the forest floor. Tobin stuck his head back inside the log. Mercifully, no websacks lined the edges of the opening, so nothing squirmed beneath his paws just yet. But as he and Wiley stepped farther inside, sticky, squishy ooze gushed through their toes. Chunks of some kind poked his paw pads beneath it all, and he forced his mind to not solve that riddle.

Don't look down, just look ahead.

He stared ahead. And gagged. His recently eaten earthworm threatened to come back up as he stared at row upon row of websacks in front of him.

Wiley crawled beside him. His friend's lips curled in disgust. "You check the sacks on this side, and I'll do the other?"

Tobin nodded. He took one step forward, the soppy floor belching as he pulled his paw from the goop. Three small steps later, a shadow flicked across the floor—then he saw them: long, spindly leg shadows marching in his direction.

The cries, clicks, chirps, and squeaks surrounding them fell silent.

"Wiley, hide!" Tobin hissed and pressed himself against the tunnel wall, wedging between a clump of websacks. He saw Wiley do the same.

He closed his eyes. *Sludge, sludge, sludge, sludge . . .*

The sacks around him began to squirm. He shut his eyes tighter. The sack inhabitants poked at him. They investigated him, feet and feelers rubbing him through their webbed cases.

The sound of slurping echoed down the tunnel, followed by a faint scraping. Then the sounds ceased. Slowly, the cacophony of chirping, crying, hissing, and squeaking captives began again. The Arakni must have done its work and scuttled on.

Tobin cracked his eyes open. Before he could stop himself, he looked to the source of the pressure against his cheek. A tiny foot.

A baby toad. Four skinny toes, all different lengths, pushed against its unnatural cocoon.

Tobin gasped and stumbled away from the wall, slime sticking to his fur. But he couldn't tear his eyes from the tiny toad, which now pressed its head against the translucent barrier. Its jeweled eyes pleaded for help.

A voice from behind almost sent Tobin through the ceiling.

"We should free them all."

Tobin whirled around to see Wiley. A half-starved hummingbird sat cradled in his front paws. Wiley shuffled to a crack in the log. Stretching on his hind legs, he placed the trembling creature on narrow splinter of wood. The tiny bird rolled onto its feet and flicked its wings. After a few shaky starts, it fluttered out.

A thrill of joy and a rash of fury rolled through Tobin. His mind was torn in two. He didn't want to alert the Arakni they were here by freeing everyone. But he wanted nothing more than to pull that toad off the wall.

Well, that wasn't exactly true. There *was* something he wanted more.

"Fine," he answered Wiley. "After we find the pinkling, we rip down all these websacks."

twenty

A PINKLING IS BLIND.

It's completely helpless, without any fur. Totally, well, *pink*. Unlike the baby toad or hummingbird, the pinkling needed Tobin's strong legs and sharp eyes to make an escape. He reminded himself of this as he passed by countless creatures staring at him for help.

"I'll be back, I'll be back," he muttered as he sloshed past the forlorn faces.

Another set of shadows stretched across the tunnel floor. Again, Tobin slid alongside the wall. The websacks he wriggled between pressed back against him, enclosing him.

Hiding him. Like the creatures knew he was their only hope to escape.

Rule #9: Never expect a creature who still draws breath to go down without a fight, for all creatures' first instinct is to survive.

Tobin closed his eyes and waited, letting the webbed critters pull him into their embrace. After a few moments, the usual chorus of chirps and buzzes signaled the all clear. The pressure lifted from his back, his head, and his legs. Somewhere, something unclamped his tail.

"Thanks," Tobin whispered before slinking down the tunnel. He approached the most recent returning point of the hunting spiders. The websacks here were all shinier, the prisoners more restless than the others. Tobin pressed his nose to a silk case. It was stickier. Yes. These were fresher. This is where he'd find his pinkling.

He surveyed the captives, then plodded a few more steps. As he peered through the gray webbed prisons, he began to feel frantic. The pulsing sacks started to blur together. And the sheer stink of the place made his nose useless. He shut his eyes.

Calm down. Focus, or this is all for nothing.

Then he heard it. Somehow, between the clicks and chirps, he heard a very breathy squeak.

He opened his eyes. He tilted his head and his ears perked. He could think of only one thing to do.

He *tchir*red.

Loudly.

If insects could gasp, they might have. The tunnel

206

fell silent. Hearing nothing, Tobin breathed in until he thought his chest would burst. *"Tchirrrr, tchirrrr!"*

Quiet. Until a moment later.

"Eep, eep."

A sound so faint it was watery—Tobin almost missed it. Almost. His head snapped right, his gaze lingering over a half dozen sacks, until . . . *there!*

The websack was just the right size, but it was spun so thick its occupant was hidden.

Tobin trudged to the wall. Stretching up, he threaded his paws behind the sack, tearing the spongy binding away. Putting one paw under the bundle, he curled his other behind the sack. He tugged gently, stumbling back as the final cords of webbed binding snapped from the wall. Paws shaking, he stared. Even through the thickly wound strands of silk, warmth ebbed into Tobin's paw pads as the tiny occupant wriggled.

Tobin buried his muzzle into the webbing and sniffed. He heard a soft sniffle inspecting him in return. A sweet scent, like milk and dandelions, flooded his nostrils, and Tobin's head swam with emotion. His pinkling. *Their* pinkling. All the Arakni stench in the world couldn't erase the smell of home.

The chant of creatures waiting to be freed buzzed

in his ears, and another *tchirr* echoed down the tunnel. Wiley had heard him and was coming.

Tobin looked at the bundled pinkling, his paws shaking. "We'll get you home soon," he whispered just as Wiley approached. Tobin turned and saw Wiley wasn't alone.

"Talia! What are you doing in here?"

She didn't answer as her stare fixed on the webbed bundle. "Oh." She stretched out a paw, caressing the websack. "Hi, little one, you okay in there?"

"I think the cocoon keeps the pinkling warm," Tobin said. "As much as I hate it, we should leave the baby in there for now."

A smile flickered across Wiley's face, but vanished as soon as he spoke. "Hess sent Talia to find us. The owls have arrived. There's about a dozen or so waiting on the branches outside. Hess is waiting for us back at the opening."

Talia nodded excitedly. "The owls swooped and squished the last couple Arakni that tried coming in here. And no, Hess doesn't think the owls are necessarily helping us, they're just bored waiting for the snakes to get here."

Tobin's mind spun like a rat chasing its tail. "Then

we have a little time. I say we start ripping down these websacks. Maybe we can't fight the Arakni quite like the snakes and owls, but we can still hit 'em where it hurts."

Wiley flicked his tail. "Yeah. Let's free their food supply."

Talia nuzzled the webbed bundle, and the pinkling cooed. She held out her paws. "Told you I was big enough to help. I can carry the pinkling out of here."

Tobin handed her the newborn. "You were right. Be safe."

"I will. You too." She tucked the bundle under one paw and scooted through the grime with a three-legged shuffle.

Tobin and Wiley slopped through the muck till they reached the farthest end of the fallen tree, finding the very first row of sacks. "Ready?" Tobin asked.

Wiley locked his front paws together, stretching every muscle from his toes to his shoulders. "Yup. With the owls taking out any spiders near the entrance, these captives have a chance to escape."

Tobin flipped his paw, claws curling up. "You get that side. I'll get this one." Then he pounced.

Like a filthy cyclone of teeth and claws, Tobin slashed and ripped at the underbellies of the sacks. He tore gashes big enough for captives to scratch, kick, and squirm their way through. Toads tumbled to the floor. Slugs slipped into the muck. Tobin barely felt the thrum of dragonfly wings against his head or centipedes winding through his legs, as he yanked row after row of sacks from the wall. Every now and then, he'd kick and scratch holes in the rotten tunnel wall, allowing the smallest captives to escape without fighting through the gloppy floor.

His legs burned as he neared where Talia waited with the pinkling. She'd done some damage herself; the sacks around her lay torn to shreds. She stood on her hind legs, letting a tiny, twig-sized snake wind its way up her back toward the opening.

Tobin's chest caved in and out as he caught his breath. He watched the snake crawl into the sunlight. Another victim freed. Causing trouble for the Arakni was all the fuel Tobin needed. He crouched next to his sister. "Climb up."

Talia smiled and stepped onto his back. Reaching high, she set the pinkling on the ledge and hoisted herself out.

Tobin watched her go until the very tip of her tail was out of the log. Then he reached for the next row of sacks, sending a nearly dried-out salamander and a handful of potato bugs slipping to the ground.

As he reached to yank another row from the wall, a growl caught his attention. He peered ahead and his heart sank. Wiley, standing a little farther down the tunnel, was staring down two Arakni hunters who towered over him, as tall as cardinals.

"Wiley!" Tobin yelled. He pushed hard, sloshing toward his friend as fast as possible. Wiley's fur spiked from his shoulders all down his backbone, and his jaws snapped as he snarled. But the hulking Arakni made it impossible to escape around them, and with the goo-covered floor, there was no outrunning them, either.

Tobin neared Wiley's side, and the spiders rocked back and forth on their long legs. Their patches of red eyes quivered. Little creatures were doing their best to scramble around the spiders' legs, but the spiders looked unsure which dilemma to address: the snarling, muck-covered rodents or their quickly escaping food supply. Tobin's throat went dry as his gaze fell upon the Arakni mouths. Like pits surrounded by a hundred curling crab legs, able to seize hold of *anything*.

"Uh-oh. They must be on patrol duty," said Tobin.

"Should we pounce?" asked Wiley.

Tobin tensed, blood pumping through his muscles.

"Don't think we have much choice. Go for their eyes, and use the wall."

The floor was too sticky for jumping, so Tobin lunged to the side, his paws finding footholds in the shredded websacks. He could see Wiley doing the same. The spiders took a step forward, and Tobin scrambled along the sidewall until he was almost in reach of the Arakni. But before the Arakni could throw out a sharp-tipped leg, Tobin pounced.

He pushed off the wall, his extra adrenaline giving him more boost than he ever had before. He flew over the head of one spider, dodging the leg it threw up in defense, and raked his claws across its head. Tobin dug in hard when he felt the soft, squishy eyes beneath his paws.

The spider bucked, and its hard-shell back connected with Tobin, sending him directly into a wall. The remnants of websacks softened the impact, but he still felt a throbbing in one leg.

The spider spun on him. He craned his neck around the approaching spider to see that Wiley was regaining his bearings after being thrown to the ground as well. They'd each landed a blow on their respective Arakni, but at what cost?

The spiders flung their long front legs outward, probing. *They can't see us,* Tobin realized. Yet another wild idea popped into his head.

Without thinking too hard about what he was about to do, Tobin sprang into the air, his mouth open wide. He reached his paws up, clutching one of the spider's waving legs. He brought it down to his mouth and bit. Hard.

A satisfying *crunch* sounded in his ears. Landing in the muck, Tobin squeezed the now-separated appendage in his paws.

"Atta way, Tobin," he heard Wiley call from across the tunnel, where Wiley was keeping his spider occupied by hopping from the walls onto its back, landing blows, and repeating.

Tobin's spider was now thoroughly enraged. It reared back, ready to stab Tobin through with all its available legs. But rearing back was a mistake.

Tobin saw an opening, a soft spot in the Arakni's underbelly, where the spider vented air in through its abdomen. That was his target.

But the muck was thick, and Tobin couldn't pounce. Instead he raised his spider-leg spear, holding his ground until the Arakni came down, bringing its full force directly on Tobin.

Tobin braced himself, but the momentum of the falling spider was more than he imagined. A jarring impact shook his whole body as the spider fell onto the spear, then something gave way, and the spear slid through. Everything went black as the spider's body fell on him. It pressed Tobin down, deep into the sludge on the tunnel floor. He was pinned beneath the deadweight of the Arakni's body. Tobin gasped for air, but the sludge was threatening to swallow him whole.

Just as he was fighting for breath, he felt a pinch on his shoulder, and then a yank. And another, until finally there were two paws grabbing and pulling on his shoulders.

"C'mon," grunted Wiley. "I've . . . got . . . you!"

With a final pull, Wiley wrenched Tobin free, and the two of them were flung backward against the tunnel wall.

"Whoa." Wiley was panting, then looked to Tobin. "You took down a hunter spider!"

Tobin nodded, a bit in disbelief himself. Then a moment of panic. "Where's the spider you were fighting?"

"Oh, I think I drove him nuts. He stumbled out that way." Wiley jerked his head in the direction of the tunnel opening, and Tobin saw Wiley's right eye was swollen shut.

"Wiley! Your eye." Tobin sat up, worry for his friend reenergizing him.

"Yeah." Wiley wiped a paw over the right side of his face. "That Arakni got one lucky swipe, but that's it."

"Can you walk okay?" Tobin asked as they got to their feet.

"I think so, just a little dizzy." Wiley stood and stretched out his legs, testing for good measure. "Yup, just a little dizzy. And, you know, can't see the best."

Tobin glanced down the tunnel at the remaining websacks, the occupants still wriggling, desperate for their freedom. He nodded and swallowed the lump in his throat. "Okay, you need to head back to Hess and Talia. I'll get the rest of these down."

Wiley began to shake his head, but soon wobbled on his feet. Tobin steadied him with a paw. "Wiley, seriously. Start heading out. There's only a few sacks left."

Wiley winced. "Yeah, okay." He stepped toward the opening. "Be careful, Tobin."

"I will." Tobin turned, stepping over to the remaining sacks. "Did you hear that?" he asked the cricket, snail, and ladybug he let loose. "Wiley just told *me* to be careful. Strange times indeed!"

twenty-one

NO MORE INTERRUPTIONS. NO more Arakni or vipers or owls. Just Tobin, alone. He'd worked his way toward the far end of the fallen tree, near the canopy. There'd been hundreds of websacks when they'd started; now he was down to the final captives.

He tugged down a particularly lumpy bundle, and barely ducked the back end of a very feisty wasp as it wriggled free. Tobin leaned back until the wasp completely pulled itself out of the sack and buzzed away.

I just dodged a wasp sting. Before yesterday, dodging a wasp would've been all he talked about for weeks. Now he'd need to add an extra season to the year to get through talking about this one horrific place.

As he turned back to free the last few creatures, his rear paw slid into an opening in the floor, right where

216

the wall hit the ground. He jumped back and looked down. A crevice ran the length of a squirrel's tail, from where he stood right to the end of the log. Though he knew better, Tobin thought maybe the log had just rotted out, but he crouched lower for a look anyway.

Speckles of dirt and wood fibers mixed with the slop that coated the floor. A tingle spread from his cheeks to his feet. This pit was dug intentionally. But why?

Tobin sighed and looked up, though there was no sky to gaze upon and contemplate, only rotting wood. He'd come this far. He needed to know what was down there. No unanswered questions. Tobin drew in a deep breath, then stuck his head down the hole.

Almost pitch-black. So dark Tobin closed his eyes to speed along their adjusting.

When he opened them again, what he saw made his nose go ice cold. As neatly as the websacks were laid out in rows above, Arakni egg sacks were nestled in the dugout below. The perfect circles gave them away. Tobin had seen spider eggs before, but never hundreds of them together like this. And *never* walnut-sized. Tobin squinted. Maybe it was the tremors of his heart pounding, but it looked like the spheres pulsed. The websacks had been the food for these hatchlings.

Were they ready to hatch? Maybe he was okay with leaving one unanswered question at the rotting log.

Tobin whipped his head out of the dank chamber. His friends needed him, the last row of websacks needed him. He continued pulling. A moth fluttered away. Some beetles he couldn't identify scuttled off, and the final sack held a vertebrate—a leopard frog no bigger than a grape, still equipped with a tadpole tail.

Food for the Arakni young. Tobin shook his head and sagged against the wall. He watched the remaining creatures escape, each instinctively fleeing toward a crack in the log where a sliver of sun crept through.

Sun. Fresh air. Freedom.

Exhausted and sticking to the wall, Tobin rocked himself until he slumped free. The closeness of the sunbeam was tempting, but he knew that wasn't *his* way out. He needed to go farther back down the log tunnel, to where his friends waited. Where Hess stood by, ready to take them away from spiders, owls, and other snakes that lurked outside. So, he walked, one last time through the slop, until he finally saw his exit.

The corners of his mouth twitched. He almost smiled, but was too tired. Only a few steps and he could join his friends and take their pinkling home. He stretched his paws and began his climb. But just then a hot, searing pain shot through his hind leg.

He cried out, his claws digging into the wall. He looked down. Something black speared his leg, right below his hip. He traced the length of the long harpoon. It was a leg. And it was connected to an Arakni.

Tobin could barely catch his breath. *Speared.* Like a fish skewered on a heron's beak.

Tobin tried to call, but his dry throat only croaked out a whisper. "Hess," he tried again, never breaking his gaze from the blood-red eyes watching him.

Its mouth pincers curled, beckoning him closer.

With muscles fueled by panic, Tobin managed to drag himself toward one of the cracks in the wall, but then the Arakni yanked his leg. Tobin screamed as red-hot stinging pain washed over him. His head began to swim and he remembered: *the venom!* He dug his claws deeper into the soft wall, but it offered little resistance as the Arakni pulled him down. The sunlit opening grew farther from his grasp.

He'd been *so close*.

Then, from above, a forked tongue flicked inside the log and smacked his forehead, just as the spider yanked— hard. Tobin flew across the tunnel, his breath suddenly crashed from his lungs as the spider slammed him onto the spongy floor. On his back and wheezing, he saw a blurry version of himself fly through the air and land atop the Arakni's abdomen. But that wasn't right, he was lying on the ground, he wasn't fighting the spider, unless—Tobin cleared his eyes and saw the spider twisting around, legs swiping madly . . . at Wiley. With his back legs wrapped around the Arakni's midsection, Wiley dangled over the spider's side and furiously chomped at the leg that had speared Tobin. With a *crunch*, the leg broke free from the spider and fell into the muck. Tobin stared at the lost appendage, which mercifully tugged at him no more— but still weighed him down. If only he could pry himself off the jagged leg spear, he could escape. But his limbs, they felt . . . *heavy*. He could barely raise a paw. And the floor was so sticky.

An explosion of light blinded him, and Tobin lolled his head sideways to see a black snout crashing through the decayed wood. Ivory teeth snapped at the spider until they found their mark. Hess severed the Arakni's head and spit it to the floor. The Arakni's body convulsed as it crumpled to the ground, its appendages still quivering.

Wiley appeared at his side; his face looking perhaps even more swollen than before. Tobin felt sick—he wanted to throw up, wanted some fresh air. But he was a lump of stiff clay; he couldn't even swipe his tail.

"Hang in there," said Wiley, "just need to get that stinger out. This will only hurt a second."

A sting shot through Tobin's hip as Wiley pulled the Arakni appendage from his leg.

Pain. Like a hundred hornets stinging his leg, as Wiley ripped the barbed leg tip from his hip. He heard a scream; it might have been him. But he could barely open his mouth.

Come to think of it, he could barely breathe.

Tobin felt himself lifted from the ground. Hess. The snake had scooped him into his mouth, tucking him behind the fangs into its warm, fleshy center.

Bright sunlight glared in Tobin's half-open eyes as Hess brought him out of the log and lowered him on his back. Wiley scrambled to meet him, looping his paws under his shoulders, gripping him tight.

"What happened to him?" Tobin heard Talia ask, her voice quivering.

"Hang on tight to the pinkling," was Hess's only answer. "We have to go. I'll try and slide us around the battle."

Tobin felt a tickle on his leg. Talia was sniffing his

wound. "We need to get him to a clean puddle," she said.

Hess slid away from the log. "There will be plenty at the base of the hill. But it'll be slow moving. I'm going to try and avoid interlopers."

"Interwhat?" said Wiley.

"Meddlers. Like Swallfyce. Or worse—my mother."

Since his face happened to be pointing up and he couldn't move, Tobin looked skyward. Owls flew in and out of his sight line, putting on a fascinating show. They'd swoop and then come up with an Arakni in their claws. They'd scrunch it, sending bits of glop falling to the ground. The sounds of jaw snaps and hisses swirled around Tobin's head.

Something violet streaked alongside them for a few moments. Another snake. It raised its nose, inspecting Tobin, still held firmly by Wiley. It hissed something he couldn't understand, and Hess hissed something in reply, before it slithered away.

They rode quietly down the hill. The sounds of screeches and hisses grew more distant. Every now and then Hess would jerk left or right. Wiley and Talia took turns saying things like, "We've got you," and "We're almost there."

Almost where? They weren't almost home. No, there

was the matter of a crossing a gorge and a creek.

He felt a tingle in his paw. An icy prickle broke across his face, and Tobin twitched his nose. A shudder of spasms ran down his back.

"Hey," Wiley called, "I think the venom's wearing off!"

A torrent of tingles peppered his body like raindrops. Whatever it was, at least it was ebbing away. Tobin closed his eyes, waiting for the tingles and twitches to run their course. He felt no more as he drifted to sleep.

If not for the splashes of water, Tobin could've slept longer.

Water? Where was he? "Catfish," he muttered, his body flinching. A sharp pain in his hind leg helped pop his eyes wide open.

Talia spoke. "No catfish, Tobin. You're in a puddle."

He blinked water from his eyes. Sure enough, he lay soaked to the bone, his chin resting at the edge of a puddle. He raised his head and looked over his shoulder. Talia cupped water in her paw and poured it over his wound.

Wiley hop-stepped beside her, the pinkling cradled in one front leg. His cheek still looked like it was over-stuffed with seeds, but at least his eye was cracked open.

"We all needed a good rinse. Except for this little guy. And we needed to clean out your leg. How're you feeling?"

Sore. Everywhere. And his leg throbbed. At least he could feel it. "Better, I guess."

Both Wiley and Talia's foreheads creased with skeptical looks.

Sitting up on her haunches, Talia tapped a hind leg. "Really? From what I hear, you were harpooned, poisoned, and body slammed."

"Okay, fine, I'm sore." Tobin propped himself up on his front legs. "But since I couldn't even *move* a while back, I'd say I'm at least a little better."

"Hmm." Wiley scratched his chin. "Try walking."

Talia's eyes bulged. "Are you sure about that?"

Wiley nodded. "Yeah. We need to know where he stands. Like, really. We need to know *if* he can stand."

Tobin pushed up on his three strong legs. He curled his injured leg beneath him. "Ouch" slipped out before he could stop it, and Talia jumped forward.

"No, wait, I can do this." Gritting his teeth, Tobin hopped with his good hind leg, stepping with his front two. "Well, I can move, anyway." He step-hopped out of the puddle. "Where's Hess?"

"Hess is getting us some food." Talia jerked her head. "There's a mulberry bush over there. Hess said he won't venture far from us now, since we're all washed off and look appetizing again."

A branch snapped, and a moment later Hess appeared, dragging a berry-laden limb. Tobin's stomach rumbled.

Hess skidded the buffet of berries before them. "Glad to see you're up, Tobin. Some energy should do you wonders. I've always heard rodents are notoriously fast healers. Now I can see for myself."

Talia reached out, yanking a plump, plum-colored fruit off the stem. "Hmmm . . . maybe it'd be easier if we made a pile for you."

Tobin smiled gratefully, needing his three good legs for balancing, not berry picking. He snatched a berry off the ground, his jaws chomping the juicy morsel. He swallowed a bite and could practically feel his body sucking up the nutrients. Food was a great idea.

Food! The urgency of his own thought almost tipped Tobin over. "The Arakni log—the websacks—it was all like a horrible nursery."

A mulberry dropped from Wiley's mouth. "Umm, what?"

"Beneath the log"—Tobin shook his head and steadied

his voice—"I saw a hole in the floor of the log. So I looked down, and there was a huge, excavated chamber full of Arakni eggs. Row after row. The captives in the websacks were supposed to be food for the hatchling Arakni."

Hess, Wiley, and Talia stared at him in silence for a moment before Talia finally spoke what they all were thinking. "Do you think the snakes and owls found the eggs?"

Hess looked back up the hill. "I have no idea."

"Well, either way"—Wiley picked up his dropped mulberry—"there's not going to be anything for those little buggers to eat if they do hatch."

"Thank goodness you two freed everyone," said Talia.

Hess nodded. "Speaking of eating, please eat more, Tobin. And then we need to get moving."

"Right." Tobin took another bite of berry and spoke between chomps. "Where are we, anyway?"

Hess turned his head into the breeze, his tongue flicking in and out. "Near the gorge, about ten hare-leaps from Hubbart's."

Tobin's half-full belly pinched with nerves. "Hubbart . . . I hope he's okay. I hope he'll forgive us."

"We can worry about his forgiveness later." Hess

narrowed his eyes. "The battle on the Arakni hilltop will be over soon. The spiders were scattering even as we made our way down the hill."

Tobin cocked his head. "That's good, right? The Arakni got knocked down a few pegs in the hunting order. The balance should be better all over the woods."

"Yes," said Hess, "that part is very good. But the snakes will be ready to return home. And how, do you suppose, they will proceed?"

Tobin looked at Wiley and Talia. Their grim faces told Tobin they already knew the answer. "They're going back to Hubbart's tunnels."

Hess nodded. "It's a familiar path, and one they know is safe. Only this time, they'll be starving."

twenty=two

AFTER A COUPLE OF unsuccessful boosts from Wiley, Tobin gave in. "All right, *fine.*"

Hess plucked him up by the scruff of his neck and dropped him astride his back. Tobin gripped tight with his front paws, letting his injured leg hang over the side.

Wiley had insisted Tobin ride in front, saying, "If you fall, we might not be able to catch you, but at least we'll see you slip and won't leave you in the dust." It wasn't the most comforting thought, but Tobin couldn't argue.

Wiley and Talia sat behind him, taking turns holding the pinkling.

Hess glanced back. "Everyone ready?"

Tobin nodded and Hess slid forward. They whooshed along the edge of the gorge, choosing speed over the safety of traveling under cover. The rocky path was a very straight shot to Hubbart's.

"We're getting close," Hess called back. "And Tobin, if you fall—fall to the left."

No kidding, Tobin thought as he peeked into the gorge. Far below, a few fleeing Arakni scuttled across the canyon floor. Where would they go? To find a new home? Or eventually retreat back to their rotten log when this was all over?

"There!" Talia jolted Tobin from his thoughts. Looking over Hess's head, a familiar grassy knoll rested between the woods and the gorge. Tobin shivered. The entrance to Hubbart's den seemed a lot different from this view. The granite slab jutting from the ground looked like the stretched-open jaws of a snake.

He turned to Talia and Wiley to see if they saw it, but they were both entranced with the cooing pinkling. Then again, Tobin was the only one who'd been snapped up in snake jaws recently. Maybe they wouldn't even notice the similarity.

Hess slid to a stop beside the granite slab.

"Hey." Wiley poked Tobin with his tail. "You need help getting down?"

"No, I can do this." *Gravity will be help enough*, he thought. Curling his injured leg beneath him, Tobin slipped headfirst over Hess's side. His front legs supported his weight, and he planted his good hind leg a moment later. Pain pinched his thigh from the jolt, but the sting didn't last long.

Hess sniffed around the perimeter of the den and shook his head. "There's snake scent everywhere—multiple serpents. I can't begin to imagine how many."

"Dozens, if ya do care to know, ya rapscallion!"

Tobin's head snapped up. "Hubbart!"

The woodchuck now sat atop the granite slab, glaring at them with narrowed eyes. "I've been watching for you shysters." The growl in his voice was unmistakable.

Talia clapped her front paws together. "Hubbart, thank goodness you're safe."

"*Safe?*" Hubbart blinked and pointed his nubby paw. "If by *safe* you mean not digesting in a snake's belly, then sure! But if you think an entire gaggle of unwelcome reptilians slitherin' through my den has left my family feeling *safe*, you are one pitifully mistaken mouse!"

Talia bit her lip before continuing. "We're so sorry, Hubbart, we didn't know—"

"Now that's rich!" Hubbart threw his paws in the air. "Oh, you're a clever one, all right! Rubbing yer scent all over, saying it would deter predators, not attract them!"

A vein on Hubbart's forehead throbbed so hard Tobin saw it pounding. Probably best to speak extra politely. "Please, Hubbart, the snakes used us to find the spiders.

We didn't know! We're sorry they followed us here, but—"

"But what?" the cross woodchuck snarled. "Aye, the serpents had a mission on their minds, or they'd have hunted my family. But that doesn't make what you did all right. Don't even think about using my tunnels again. No way, no how!"

"Enough!" Hess growled. He slithered forward, raising his head to the height of the perched woodchuck. He stared at Hubbart eye to eye. "We haven't time for this. The snakes will be returning soon."

Hubbart's nose crinkled. He batted a pebble with his paw. "I knew it! I knew those infernal serpents would be back, shovin' and a-bullying—"

Hess nodded impatiently. "Yes, they will. Your warren provides the simplest, safest path of descent back into the gorge."

Hubbart's chest puffed, his bottom lip stuck out in a scowl.

Hess continued. "These mice knew nothing of the snakes' plan. *Nothing.* Look for yourself. They're carrying the very pinkling they sought to rescue."

Hubbart flicked his gaze past Hess, and Talia raised the bundle. The woodchuck's eyes softened for a moment, but when he looked back to Hess, Hubbart's eyes hardened to black stones. "But you, snake. What of your role in this?"

"I didn't know the snakes were following us until it was too late."

Hubbart rolled his eyes. Hess's lips curled back and he continued. "Look, I don't care if you believe me or not. I'm not asking you for anything. But the mice—please, let the mice hide deep in your warren until the snakes pass back through."

Tobin's ear twitched. Did he hear that right? "What about you, Hess? Where are you going to be?"

"I'll wait out here."

Alone? The thought sent a shiver down Tobin's spine. "No, that doesn't seem safe."

"It's the best way," Hess answered before looking back to Hubbart. "I'll try and dissuade the snakes from causing you and your family any harm."

Hubbart rested his cheek on a curled paw. "Oh, come on. Yer a big fella, but why would a whole slew of hungry snakes abide by you?"

"I do have some pull with their queen," said Hess. "And, I could offer them a helpful bit of information."

Hubbart scrunched his forehead. "Like what?"

"You know this territory. Tell me the best way for the snakes to travel back up the other side. I'll guide the snakes back across the gorge myself, away from your den, on the condition that they leave you all alone."

"Interesting." Hubbart rubbed his chin.

Talia leaped in front Hess. "I don't think so! What if the snakes don't agree to your terms? Remember disobeying your mother? And not being Favored anymore?"

Hubbart rubbed his brow. "I hate to say it, but the lass is right. There's nooks in the den perfect for ambushing no-good reptiles. If those snakes decide to come in the den looking for a meal, we'd hold 'em off in the tunnels far easier than you gettin' swarmed out here, all by yer lonesome."

Hess shook his head slowly. "No. No more snakes in your den. I need to do this. I know I have some allies among these snakes—friends, even. I'll try getting them across, and if all goes well, I'll be waiting for you in the gorge tomorrow morning."

"No—" Tobin started, but Hubbart cut him off.

"Agreed, snake." The woodchuck hopped from down the stone. "I'll show ya an easy path for yer brethren to slither up the other side. Just don't let any of the vermin inside me home."

"So now we're spending the night?" Wiley asked.

Hess nodded. "I don't know how long the snakes will linger. And Tobin needs to rest his leg, and you should put some yarrow on that eye. And everyone needs sleep." Hess turned and followed Hubbart to the ridge of the gorge.

Tobin threw his paws in the air. "Don't we get a say in this?"

"Ahem!"

Tobin spun around. Another woodchuck with curiously long eyelashes peeked at the mice from beneath the slab. "So yer the mice that led that army of snakes through my home?"

Talia's whiskers twitched. "That's not exactly what—"

"Never mind. I heard yer whole chat out here. Seems me husband has struck another deal." The woodchuck raised a brow. "My name's Nuna. Now, let's get you inside and hope yer serpent friend is good for his word."

"He is." Tobin looked over his shoulder. Hubbart was pointing out landmarks to Hess near the ridge. *Can we really leave him out here?*

Nuna clucked her tongue. "No dallying now. I bet that pinkling's famished, the poor dear."

Tobin looked at the little webbed bundle. "You're right."

Nuna nodded and ducked into the tunnel, raising her voice for the mice to hear. "We'll head to the nursery, plenty of milk and turnips. And yarrow for you two scrappers."

Talia followed behind her, then Wiley. Tobin glanced back one last time. "See you in the morning," he said under his breath to Hess, who was still intently listening to Hubbart. Tobin turned and followed his friends into the labyrinth of tunnels.

Hubbart had called it the "belly o' the den." It felt that way. Ascending, descending, curving—like winding through the hillside's intestines. They wove around tree roots and shards of rock. On most days, Tobin felt more relaxed in tunnels, tucked safely away from the world. But now his mind buzzed with too much worry. He was safe from the outside dangers and elements, but Hess wasn't.

"Tut, tut, keep up, little mouse. This teeny babe needs to eat," Nuna chided him.

His worrying interfered with his hobbling and he'd fallen behind. *Hess knows what he's doing,* Tobin assured himself and quickened his hop-stepping, earning a sympathetic look from Talia.

The snake briefly slipped from Tobin's mind once Nuna led them to a cavernous room. It was lit by a single beam of bluish light, no thicker than a walnut. It pierced the darkness from the peak of the room.

Tobin's jaw dropped. "How'd you get light down here?" He cocked an ear and stepped toward the beam. "We've got to be three cattail reeds deep. And this hole—it's so narrow." He craned his neck, squinting in the light. "You couldn't have dug this."

"An industrious little mole dug it years ago." Nuna shuffled over beside him. "The mole's long gone, so every now 'n' again the kids'll catch a digger beetle and toss it up there. The little buggers scuttle up and out, keeping the light shaft clear for us."

Tobin nodded. "Great idea."

From behind, an unfamiliar voice chimed, "Thanks."

Tobin turned, blinking away the blue haze. Seven pairs of dark eyes materialized from the stubbly brown wall. The woodchuck litter!

"Oh." Tobin stepped back. "Sorry, I didn't see you."

The sandy-colored woodchucks smiled and chattered, looking at each other approvingly. One sat back on his haunches. "That's because we blended into the wall. It's a trick."

Another kit nodded. "Yup, Dad calls it *cam-o-fla-shing*." More giggles.

"Can you do it again?" Talia asked.

An echo of "Sure, sure!" bubbled down the line of little kits. Tobin realized the kits only *looked* little because they were miniature versions of Hubbart and Nuna. They were already twice Tobin's size.

Nuna clucked her tongue, speaking to the kits on her

right. "After ya show off yer tricks, Jax, Milly, and Sal—please pull out a turnip and some yarrow mash for our guests." The kits nodded, then Nuna addressed those on her left. "Luc, Giddy, Cape, and Bebby—show the mice where they can hunker down for the night."

They nodded in unison, and Nuna looked to Talia. The mother woodchuck smiled, her long eyelashes curling into her forehead. "Why don't you let me tend to the pinkling a while, dear?"

The gentleness of Nuna's voice reminded Tobin of his own mom—he could only imagine how frightened she was at this point. Now a boulder of worry for his mom plunked down alongside his concern for Hess.

Talia gave the bundle a nuzzle, then handed the baby to Nuna. When Talia turned around, the kits had frozen themselves to the wall. Eyes closed, their speckled fur blended flawlessly.

Talia clapped her paws. "That's amazing!"

Seven sets of eyes popped open. Three kits tumbled away to fetch a turnip. The other four showed them where to sleep. A small alcove dug into the wall would fit three mice perfectly. "We used to put acorns in there," one of the kits explained—maybe Bebby?

When the turnip arrived, they ate and chatted. Talia and Wiley did most of the talking. The kits asked Talia if they could keep her, promising they would take great care of her. She politely said no, but promised to visit.

Nuna returned with the pinkling cradled in one front arm. There was a hole in webbing, and the pinkling's wrinkly little face showed through.

Talia gasped, and Wiley and Tobin grinned as they scurried to see the newborn.

"I hope ya don't mind," Nuna said softly, "but I had to peel away a little web to nurse the babe. He's quite comfortable now, but I'm sure he'd rather sleep cozied up with you all."

Tobin's heart skipped a beat. "Did you say 'he'?"

Nuna smiled, again losing half her lashes in her forehead. "Yes, sweetie. A baby boy."

"Told ya." Wiley nudged Talia.

"I don't care, he's perfect!" she squealed, reaching up for the bundle. Nuna placed the pinkling in Talia's arms and then ordered the onlooking kits to bed. They disappeared down a tunnel so cleverly carved into a corner Tobin hadn't noticed it. The woodchucks really were masters of camouflage.

Tobin raised his paws for a turn holding his baby brother, but Nuna shook her head. "You need rest most of all." She nudged them toward the former acorn bin.

"Remember, a good night's rest isn't just a treat—it keeps you alert upon your feet."

"Our mom says that, too," Talia said before squeaking out a yawn.

"Mom." The word slipped from Tobin's mouth.

Wiley patted him on the back. "One more night, Tobin. Then she'll be the happiest mouse this side of the moon."

"Yeah, I know," Tobin answered, but the fuzz of exhaustion clouded his brain. A tummy full of turnips and the coziness of the alcove made a perfect recipe for sleep. Tobin stumbled into a corner and plopped down. He vaguely felt Nuna pressing yarrow mash over his injured hip. As he drifted off to sleep, his last fleeting thoughts were of a green-striped snake defending a clutch of rodents against an army of serpents.

twenty-three

TOBIN DIDN'T DREAM, WHICH was just fine.
Yesterday's memories didn't really lend themselves to
pleasant dreams, anyway. So when a soft paw shook him
from his sleep, he felt surprisingly well rested.

Talia called softly, "Time to get up."

Tobin cracked open an eye. Just beyond his sister he saw
a very merry woodchuck peeking into the alcove. "Ah,
good mornin'! We were scared you were hibernating."

Tobin wiped a paw over his eyes and yawned. "Hey,
Hubbart."

"Glad you all got a good rest. Now it's midmorning
and the snake wants you home by dusk, so time to move."

A small jolt of panic zapped Tobin's sleepiness to pieces.
"Hess!"

"Is fine," Nuna called from behind Hubbart. "Just

240

waiting on you sleepyheads. I've got your pinkling here warm and fed, so grab a bite of turnip and you'll be ready to go."

Tobin crawled from the alcove into the large chamber room. Nuna held the baby, letting the kits say goodbye and look at the pinkling one last time.

Hess is safe. The pinkling is safe. Tobin sighed a breath of relief. "Thank you, Hubbart. And Nuna, for everything."

Hubbart clapped his paws. "Oh, come now. We're happy to help. Now, follow me. I'll take ya to yer serpent-in-waitin'."

"Thanks again," echoed Talia and Wiley, waving to Nuna and the kits.

Hubbart ducked into a tunnel, and the mice scampered after him. Tobin tested his injured leg as they followed, putting more and more weight on it until he found a good balance. Still a little sore—but at least he didn't have to hop on three legs all day.

Finally, Hubbart led them to the very hole they'd first used to enter his den. Hess sat curled on the gorge floor below.

"All righty, intrepid travelers," Hubbart began. "Look across the gorge. See that reddish rock there?"

Tobin nodded.

"That's where yer headed. All the serpents been using that shelf of rock to slither up and out." Hubbart raised a paw. "Swiftly and safely, be on your way."

Tobin and Talia raised a paw, and Wiley—who held the baby—raised his chin as they recited the farewell. "Swiftly and safely, till another day."

Hubbart nodded brusquely, a smile tugging at his cheeks. "Best o' luck, mice." The woodchuck shuffled a few steps deep into the tunnel before looking back. "Oh, if ya do ever return, visit me through topside tunnels. I'm caving this blasted passageway shut today."

Wiley chuckled. "I can't blame you."

Smiling, Tobin peered into the gorge, his ears pricked forward. "Hey, Hess!"

The serpent looked up, and Tobin gasped.

A purple welt the size of a walnut marred Hess's cheek. The snake's long sides blossomed with scratches.

"Oh no." Tobin scrambled down the ridge. Talia was on his heels, but Wiley lagged behind, using more caution while carrying the pinkling.

Hess tried to smile as they approached. He *tried*, but only half his face moved.

Tobin's throat went dry. "But Hubbart said you were okay."

242

"I am," Hess answered through a lopsided mouth. "I'm alive."

Wiley shielded the pinkling's eyes with a paw, which really wasn't necessary since the baby's eyes weren't open yet. "What happened?"

"There was some disagreement on the issue of using Hubbart's tunnels to reach the floor of the gorge. Or, as I saw it, to reach you all for a snack."

Tobin's eyes traced Hess's battle wounds. His stomach felt queasy. "So, while we were inside sleeping, you were out here alone, fighting for your life."

"Not alone." Hess directed his gaze at the reddish shelf of rocks. Behind clumps of roots and bramble, a dozen snakes peeked out. Sleek heads of copper, violet, green—some with stripes, some bodies blotched with the colors of the forest—all stared down at them.

Talia leaned close to Hess for protection. "Oh my."

"Don't be afraid." Hess spoke softly. "They're here to escort us. They, like me, believe you all deserve to return home safely."

Tobin drew a shaky breath. "So you're saying there was a massive snake brawl out here last night?"

Hess grinned crookedly. "Well, not the biggest snake brawl I've ever seen. But it was contentious—those snakes were hungry, after all. Honestly, the fight was just getting going when my mother arrived. Those wanting to invade Hubbart's tunnels were sent on their way—by order of the queen."

"Huh." Wiley nodded slowly, eyes shifting from roosted snake to snake. "So Tal was right. Despite everything, you're still a Favored Child with your mom." Wiley smiled lopsidedly, his grin not faring much better than Hess's with a still-swollen cheek.

Hess drew a deep breath, exhaling slowly. "I suppose, in some way, I must still amuse her."

"I knew it." Talia sat up proudly. "But no matter what your mom decreed, if it's all the same to you, Hess, you're the only snake I'll be running alongside."

"Agreed." Hess raised his head toward the new serpent lookouts. He opened his jaws and a low, rumbling hiss washed across the canyon floor. The waiting snakes called back. A chorus of hisses echoed off the walls.

The fur spiked around Wiley's shoulders. "I bet there's a hundred critters that just decided to stay home today."

The lookout snakes scattered, disappearing into the forest above. Hess slithered toward the reddish steppingstones. "Let's go."

The rock shelf made for an easy climb, even for Wiley, who continued to carry the pinkling. Once they stepped on the fringe of the forest, a rustle in the brush caught their attention. A violet-colored snake slithered out and upon seeing them, nodded and disappeared back into the thicket.

Hess turned his head to say something to the mice, but winced when the skin scrunched around the purple welt on his face. "On second thought, Talia, why don't you take the pinkling and climb aboard."

Talia looked at Tobin, worry plain on her face. "Are you sure?"

Hess nodded. "I can haul one mouseling and a pinkling. Tobin and Wiley can lead the way. Then I'm only keeping two mice in my sights, not four."

Hess's words were quick. The vibration in his voice, gone. Tobin didn't know if the others noticed, but he knew Hess was struggling. "Climb up, Tal. *Carefully.* Wiley will hand you the pinkling."

"Okay." She delicately climbed up Hess's side.

Wiley handed her the pinkling and the little bundle squealed. "We've got a happy baby today. A night at Nuna's and now I think the pinkling knows we're close to home."

"Just lead the way, and we'll arrive by sundown," said Hess.

"You've got it." Tobin padded into the forest. He slipped past familiar landmarks: the rock pile they'd slept inside that first night, the patch of forest with the huge orange toadstools. One thing was certain, it was easier moving around the woods when you were flanked by a small army of snakes.

That became Tobin and Wiley's game: snake spotting. Wiley tried "spotting" Hess, but they decided that didn't count. Most snakes were probably vines or branches, but it passed the time as they maneuvered around clumps of pine needles and leaf litter.

Wiley scratched his head. "I always thought mice were the stealthiest animals in the forest, but now I'm not sure. Snakes seem pretty sly."

Tobin nodded. "Yeah. I suppose that's the reason they pound the Rules into our heads the second we sprout fur. We have some pretty formidable enemies out here."

"Maybe." Wiley raised a brow and nodded back to Hess. "But we have some formidable friends, too. I still think a mouse can get by just following Rule Number One."

Tobin smiled.

Rule #1: Trust your first instinct.

He looked back at Talia. His sister, happily holding a web-wrapped pinkling and riding a snake. "Hey, Tal, what do you think the Rules say about snake riding?"

"Hmm," she answered. "Forget the Rules. Imagine what Mom would say!"

Tobin laughed, picturing his mom's fur turning silver instantly at the sight. "I think the Rules are more like a set of really good guidelines."

Wiley snickered beside him. "I can't believe you just said that. Don't get me wrong! I totally agree with you. I just never thought I'd hear those words out of your mouth."

"Me neither," Talia agreed. "But don't worry, Tobin, when I'm a weather scout, I'll still use the Rules, just like you."

Hess stopped his slither for a moment. "I hope I'm not out of line here, Talia, but why weather scouts? It seems like there are lots of roles to fill at your Great Burrow."

Tobin and Wiley also stopped, turning to hear the answer. A hundred possibilities suddenly filled Tobin's mind, and he realized what a great question that was.

"Well . . ." Talia paused, giving her answer some consideration. "Tobin and Wiley are the bravest, cleverest scouts ever, and that's what they do."

Tobin ears perked up at the comment, and he and Wiley exchanged looks.

"Tal," said Tobin, "that's a really nice thing to say."

"And also very true," Wiley interjected.

"Right." Tobin laughed, snatching the conversation back. "But, you know, I couldn't have been a communication scout, because I thought that class was way too hard. But you're a natural. And the plant identification—you're great at that, too. If I've learned anything on this journey, it's that you have lots of talents, and there's lots of ways you can help the burrow."

Wiley nodded in agreement. "That's true. Just keep an open mind."

"Wow." Talia looked from Wiley to Tobin, and a smile sprouted on her face. "I will. Thanks."

Wiley raised a paw. "I mean, I totally understand wanting to be like us, though."

A hiss of laughter escaped Hess. "Okay, let's get back on track here before we encourage Wiley any further."

"Definitely," Tobin chided, turning back toward the creek and smiling at his friend.

Wiley shook his head. "You know, I bet Camrik will hit the canopy when he sees us with Hess."

"Camrik?" Hess asked.

As they neared the creek, Talia told Hess all about the chipmunk. She also mentioned that the striped rodent planned on destroying the tree bridge. Hess was saying something about "delusions of grandeur" when Tobin heard the water. A moment later, he smelled it.

"We're almost there!" Glancing back to Hess, Tobin's excitement level suddenly dipped. "Um, how far are you coming with us?"

Hess flicked his tongue in and out before answering. "I've teamed up with mice, owls, and a woodchuck—may as well add a chipmunk to the list."

Tobin grinned. So close to home and he *still* didn't have to say goodbye—yet. He was a lucky mouse.

It was a quick descent through forest foliage to the cattails and bulrushes of the creek bed. Memories of a catfish and hawk flashed in his mind, and Tobin whispered, "Let's stay close together. This place is tricky."

Cautiously watching the sky and rocky surroundings, they scaled down the slope to Camrik's den. Tobin spotted the familiar, narrow entryway between rocks. "Camrik?" he called softly. "Camrik, are you in there?"

Wiley stepped in front of him and peeked inside. He sniffed. "I don't think he's home."

"Guys." Talia stood on her hind legs, balancing on Hess's head. "That's because Camrik's sitting on the stump end of the tree bridge, talking to a beaver."

Tobin's and Wiley's eyes met, and Wiley spoke first.

"A beaver! That clever rodent's really bringing down the bridge."

"Let's hurry," Hess said, speeding down the rocky slope.

They zipped through the reeds to the charred base of the tree, where the lightning strike had brought it down. Tobin raised a paw. "Wait down here a minute, Hess."

The big snake nodded, coiling beneath a clump of ferns. Talia laid the pinkling beside him.

Tobin looked up the base of the toppled tree. Standing as tall as a fawn, the tree stump looked normal. Green patches of moss still gripped its sides, the roots still firmly planted in the ground. But higher up, the scars of the lightning strike were plain to see. Streaks of black charred the wood like claw marks. Splinters of wood hung cock-eyed from the break. Tobin shivered. "If Camrik's sitting up there, out in the open, it must be safe enough to call to him, right?"

Wiley and Talia nodded, so they walked to the base of the fallen tree. They could hear the chipmunk chattering instructions to someone below in the creek. The beaver?

Tobin cleared his throat.

Tchirr! Tchirr!

Tobin waited a moment, but Camrik wasn't responding.

Tchirr—

A flash of streaked rodent flew through the air above Tobin's head.

"Yikes!" Wiley yelped, and all three mice flattened to the ground.

Camrik somehow spun midair and landed in a crouch, facing the mice, his teeth bared and his fur spiked.

Tobin held out a paw. "Camrik! It's us, remember?"

Camrik's stare crossed over each of the mice, and his chestnut coat smoothed again. "I can't believe it." He looked up at a neighboring tree. "Whole lot of good you're doing up there! These three snuck right up on me!"

A gray squirrel peered down. "You said watch for hawks."

"Squirrels," Camrik muttered, shaking his head. "Anyway." A wry smile finally crept across his face. "It is nice to see you all, and, oh." His smile disappeared. "I'm sorry you weren't able to rescue your pinkling."

"But we did," Tobin said. "He's waiting with our new friend, over there by the ferns."

"Uh-huh," Camrik said. "And why are they in the ferns?"

"Can I tell him?" Talia asked, her eyes twinkling with excitement.

"Go ahead," Tobin answered.

"Because our new friend is a snake! A real, live, fang-toothed snake. Named Hess. We thought we should warn you before he slithered out here."

Camrik raised his brow. "A snake? Okay, well, if you say so. I should tell you, I also teamed up with someone while you were gone. I wasn't sure when you would return, so I thought I should just get started on my plan."

Wiley hopped beside Tobin. "More like, he wasn't sure we *would* return."

"No kidding." Tobin pivoted his ears to take in all the sounds of the creek. One noise definitely stood out.

Scrape scrape scrape scrape scrape—CRUNCH!

Camrik climbed back up the tree stump and waved for the mice to follow.

"C'mon! Let's check it out," said Wiley.

Tobin nodded, and the three mice deftly scaled the tree trunk and sat beside Camrik, who was sitting tall and proud.

"Let's see, where'd she go . . . Ah, there." The chipmunk pointed to the water.

Tobin followed the chipmunk's gaze into the creek. The water swirled around a wriggling beaver, chomping and scraping at its point of destruction.

"Keely," Camrik called. The beaver kept working. "Keely!"

Scrape scrape—

"What?" The beaver finally called back.

Camrik jerked his head. "Come 'round a sec. These are the mice I'd told you about." Camrik hopped off the bridge where the water lapped the shoreline. Tobin lingered a moment, watching the bulky rodent smoothly slice through the water.

Talia leaped past him. "Let's go meet her." She jumped down to the water's edge and Tobin followed.

The beaver waddled partway out of the water. Her head alone dwarfed Camrik.

"Everyone, this is Keely," said Camrik. "We met when her colony was having a mushroom problem."

"That's one way to say it." She laughed. "I caught Cam stuffing his cheeks with the fungus on the dam. The mushrooms were becoming a problem, so we told him to help himself."

Camrik nodded. "I visited Keely's colony yesterday. Luckily, she thought they could use this timber downstream."

Talia sat straight up. "Then the spiders won't be able to cross again."

Keely flashed a buck-toothed smile. "That's right. Honestly, I can't stand those creepers. One of those nasty buggers tried crossing my dam once. I flattened him good with a tail flop. *Wham!*"

Keely demonstrated her tail flop, and Tobin ducked. Water exploded around them. Talia clapped as water dripped from her nose. Keely leaned closer to the mouseling. "Know what else? I left that squished spider right there, too. Just so any other creepers that came along knew what'd happen if they tried to cross my dam."

"Very clever!" said Talia.

Tobin chuckled. Talia stared at the beaver like she had a new hero.

"So." Camrik raised up onto his hind legs, peering over Tobin's shoulders. "If you all are planning to cross back over, you may want to bring out your friend and the pinkling."

"Sure, just remember, he's our friend," Tobin reminded.

"He even lets us ride him," Talia added, for good measure.

"Ride him?" Camrik folded his paws across his chest. "Just how big is this snake?"

Tobin rose onto his back legs. "Come on out, Hess."

The fern fronds shivered, and the black snake appeared, his head slithering close to the ground, a webbed bundle balanced perfectly on his snout.

"Jumpin' junipers!" Camrik sprang into the air,

landing squarely between Keely's shoulders. He peeked over the beaver's head. "I expected more of a, well, twig-sized viper."

Keely nodded. "That snake's the size of a sapling."

Wiley stepped beside Hess. "We never said he was small." Wiley reached over and took the pinkling from Hess's snout.

Hess raised his head and looked at Camrik. "My name is Hess. I'm at your disposal if I can be of any service."

"Well, my my," cooed Keely, "a real serpent *sophisticate*."

"The pinkling will need its mother soon," said Hess, "so the mice should get moving."

Tobin felt like a fish tail had just smacked his face. "Hess, don't you mean *we* should get moving?"

Keely pushed herself back into the water. "You best move then. I plan on cracking this trunk by sundown."

Hess drew a sharp breath before looking at Tobin. "Your burrow is right across the bridge, correct?"

A lump grew in Tobin's throat, so he simply nodded.

Hess continued. "Crossing a slick tree bridge can be tricky, even for nimble mice. I'm not sure how well I'd fare."

Tobin bit his bottom lip. All eyes were on him; Wiley, Talia, Hess—all waited for his response. His whiskers twitched and he cleared his throat. "I don't want to say goodbye."

Wiley lowered his gaze, grinding his paw into the dirt.

Talia jumped to Hess and flung her paws around him. "I don't want to say goodbye, either."

Hess nuzzled Talia with his good cheek. "How about this? One week from today, let's stand at this very spot on the creek. You on your side, and me on mine. We can wave our hellos."

Wiley rubbed a paw across his good eye. "That sounds good, because there is no way my brothers are gonna believe this unless they see you."

Hess gave a lopsided smile. "How about you, Tobin?"

Tobin swallowed the stone in his throat. "Okay. One week. Then we'll figure out a better way to see you."

Hess lowered his head, meeting him eye to eye. "But for now, I'll stay right here and watch you cross. Your pinkling needs your mom."

Tobin nodded, but his legs didn't seem to want to move. Talia leaned in. "Tobin, imagine how excited Mom and Dad are going to be to see us."

Tobin nodded, the thought of reuniting with his parents giving him just enough strength to say the toughest goodbye of his life. He raised his paw, and Talia and

Wiley followed suit. "Hess, my friend, swiftly and safely, be on your way."

Hess saluted in return with the tip of his tail. "Swiftly and safely, till another day. My friends."

Tobin nodded, blinking back the hot tears threatening to spill forward. *Think of Mom and Dad.* He leaned in toward Wiley, gently lifting the webbed bundle in his mouth.

"Good idea," Wiley said. "We'll need all claws on the slippery tree."

Tobin waved his tail at Camrik.

The chipmunk hollered in return, "Swiftly and safely, mice. Good luck!"

Wiley and Talia also waved their goodbyes. Tobin hopped onto the tree bridge, ready to tread its slippery surface one last time. His eyes glanced skyward. All clear, so he scurried forward, his claws providing the traction he needed. Even his injured leg wasn't bothering him much.

He focused on the bridge, the occasional laps of water that crested its sides, and the sky.

He only sensed the dark presence in the water a split second before it struck.

The clap of snapping jaws rang in his ears. A set of badger-sized claws raked the bridge.

Snapping turtle!

The creature had missed, but only by a whisker.

The beast tried again to pull its body up onto the bridge, coming between the mice and the shore. Tobin spun, tossing the pinkling from his mouth into Wiley's outstretched paws. Wiley grabbed the bundle, running back toward Camrik's shore. Tobin leaped to follow, but was jerked backward instead.

The turtle had him by the tail. With a flick of its long neck, the snapper tossed Tobin skyward. Only then, hanging midair, did he see the full form of the turtle. As wide around as a badger, its hook-beaked mouth gaped open below, its tongue wriggling in anticipation.

As Tobin fell, another open mouth streaked toward him. He shut his eyes as a hundred splinters pricked his back, and he was doused in cold creek water.

Something gripped him by the backbone, propelled him through the churning creek. He dared to open his eyes. Green water swirled as black dots peppered his vision. He needed to breathe; his mouth opened. He needed to inhale something, *anything.* Then he broke the surface. Tobin's lungs ripped the air from the sky.

A mass of brown rose to the surface beside him. "Keely?" Tobin croaked.

Keely jerked her chin up. "Put him on my back."

Clearly the beaver wasn't speaking to him. Tobin was shoved up from the water's surface, the pinch on his back releasing as he spilled onto the beaver's wet back.

Tobin flopped his head sideways. He saw Hess. The snake made eye contact with him for a moment, then slipped back into the water. Something didn't look right. Hess wasn't swimming—he was tumbling. The surging water pushed the snake downstream like a rolling strand of seaweed.

Fear clenched Tobin as Keely pressed to the shoreline. He tried to shout, but realized he was still gasping in his breaths. His vision blurred with black clouds, until the whole world went dark, one thought swirling through his mind.

Someone help Hess . . .

twenty-four

THE VOICE COMFORTED HIM.

"Hush, Tobin. My brave little hero, everything's going to be okay."

He loved that voice. It made his heart swell and his eyes flutter open. Big brown eyes gazed back at him.

Tobin blinked. "Mom?"

She smiled. "Good morning, sweetie. How are you feeling?"

Confused.

"Okay, I guess." He lifted his head from the soft grass bedding and an ache spread through his neck and shoulders. "Why do I feel . . ."

The creek. Hess. Talia.

Tobin gasped. "Mom! Where's Talia? Wiley? The baby—" His voice cracked. "Hess?"

His mom ran a paw across his forehead. "Everyone

260

is okay." She leaned her body away, revealing the baby cradled against her side. "Including your baby brother, see? He's right here. His name is Coal. And he's alive, because of you."

Tobin's thoughts seemed to drown in a sea of questions. "You and Dad, you're both okay?"

"Yes." She leaned in and clasped his paw. "When the lightning struck the tree and it fell so close to the burrow, the ground shook and caused a small cave-in. The floor in our den gave way, and we all slipped outside."

"Our den is gone?" His heart began strumming, and he felt like that hummingbird trapped in a websack.

"Everyone was able to dig out of the cave-in. The spiders took us all by surprise, and when I couldn't find the pinkling . . ." She stopped.

Tobin saw sadness filling her eyes, but she shook her head and blinked it away.

"Anyway, none of that matters now. The burrow will be fixed. And you, your sister, your brother, and Wiley, you're all home safe."

Tobin nodded, not saying anything because he sensed his mother had more to say. He was right.

"You are going to be all right, Tobin, but we do have to talk about your tail."

Tobin's breath caught in his throat. His paw slipped

to the base of his tail, clutching it gingerly. He felt it again—the pinch.

His mom set her paw over his. "Remember, you are going to be okay."

Tobin looked down; he saw his paw wrapped around the base of his tail, and his eyes traced the length of it until it stopped, but it stopped too soon.

He'd lost the tip. No, a little more than just the tip. The last third of his tail was missing.

He gasped, and his body shuddered. "Mom."

She gripped his paw more firmly. "It will take some getting used to, balance-wise, but we should be grateful it was a clean snip."

"A clean snip." A wave of sickness washed over him, and he fought to keep Nuna's turnips from reemerging. "The turtle . . . the snapper ate my tail."

"But it didn't get you, Tobin." She leaned in, pressed her forehead against his. "You're still here. That's what matters most."

Tobin lay very still, letting his mom rub his back while he took deep breaths. "You're alive, Tobin," she said softly. "Everyone you love, and everyone you fought for, is alive."

He nodded, looking around at the twigs surrounding

them, realizing this place was completely unfamiliar. "Um, where exactly are we, Mom?"

"Inside a crown shrub, just off the creek bed."

"On which side of the creek?"

"What?" She looked down, puzzled at first before understanding filled her eyes. "Our side of the creek." Her brow furrowed as she continued. "So, I should tell you there is a . . . um, beaver, running patrols every now and again, standing guard outside with your father, sister, and Wiley. And a snake. I just about had a heart attack—"

"A snake?" Tobin's heart leaped. "Black with a green stripe?"

The surprise on his mom's face melted into a smile. "Yes, Tobin. We didn't want to move you any farther, and you seem to have made a few new, interesting friends, so—"

"Mom, I have to go out there." Tobin turned. Then he turned the other way. The shrub was *really* thick.

"That way." His mom pointed. "And take it easy."

Pressing his tail flat to his body, Tobin crawled between the twigs until he saw his companions. Talia and Wiley were entertaining themselves by trying to balance on an especially large pine cone. The light of morning spilled around them. He'd been sleeping a while. "Hey," he called, wriggling free of the last spindles.

"There he is." Wiley grinned from ear to ear and hopped to his side. "Would ya look at that tail? I always thought I'd lose more pieces than you."

Tobin swerved his tail forward, examining the scabbed-over tip in his front paws. His mom was right, at least it was a clean snip.

"Crikes, Wiley," Talia scolded. "Little soon for jokes, don't ya think?"

Wiley shrugged, his paw pads up. "He's been sleeping forever. I had to wait *hours* to say that."

Tobin released his newly shortened tail. "Honestly, I always thought he'd lose more pieces, too." Tobin gave a small smile. "Hey, how's the eye?"

Wiley shrugged. "Swelling's just about gone. And if I tilt my head back, I can see just about everything, so I know it'll be okay."

"That's a relief," Tobin said. Then he looked at Talia.

She looked different, too—not physically, he realized. He saw her differently. She jumped off Lookout Landing. She never cowered from the snake queen. Or Swallfyce. She trusted Hess.

"Tal." Tobin set his paw on hers, and her huge moon

eyes looked up. "We'd have never made it without you. Not me, Wiley, or Coal."

Talia's ears and nose flushed pink. "Well, you had the idea to chase—"

"But you jumped." Tobin squeezed her paw. "You never gave up."

Talia gave a little shrug. "I have a pretty great big brother to look up to,"

Tobin released her paw and looked from Talia to Wiley. "I'm so grateful for you two."

Wiley gave a half smile, lifting his chin and nodding. "We know. We kind of like you, too."

Tobin smiled, then looked over Wiley's shoulder. "So where's Hess? Mom said—"

Just then, a booming voice demanded their attention from behind. "The adventurers are home and reunited. And my eldest adventurer has emerged."

Tobin turned to see a tan-and-black-speckled mouse walking toward them.

A smile spread across Tobin's muzzle. "Dad!"

He clasped his paws around him in a tight embrace. His dad grumbled in his ear, "Don't you ever, *ever* do anything like that again."

"I won't, Dad," Tobin answered, closing his eyes and

letting his dad squeeze some of the jitters away. Eventually Tobin looked up, and his dad loosened his grip.

"Dad, I just . . ." *Where to begin?* Tobin blinked. He'd broken the Rules. His choices put Talia and Wiley in danger. How could he explain this? "I just wanted to help. I didn't think we'd ever . . ."

"Tobin," his dad interrupted, laying his front paws on Tobin's shoulders. "Lucky for us, we'll have lots of time to talk about what you did and where the three of you went."

Tobin wanted to say more, explain things, but the lump in his throat was really getting in the way. And besides that, his dad kept talking.

"What's most important is that I know everything you did was for us. For your family."

Tobin wanted to say *That's true, it was all for the family,* but all he could manage was a nod.

"Right now," his dad whispered, "if you're up for it, I think your new friend needs your company." His dad nodded toward an overgrown fern. "He's keeping guard, as I'm told he likes to do."

Hess sat coiled in the shade, gold eyes glimmering.

Upon seeing his friend, Tobin suddenly felt like his heart was about to burst. He sniffed and cleared his throat. "Thanks, Dad." Pressing his tail to his side, Tobin walked over to the snake.

"Hess?" Tobin sat beside the big snake. There was so much to say, but one point was obvious. "For a minute I didn't think we'd make it out of that creek."

"That makes two of us," Hess answered. "But I knew Keely could carry you, once we finally reached each other."

Tobin shook his head. "It looked like the creek was going to carry you away forever."

Hess sighed. "It almost did. Almost." He smiled. "That's one quick beaver. Somehow she got you to shore, then came back into the water and found me wrapped around a piece of driftwood. I hardly remember any of it." Hess looked over to Talia and Wiley. "Honestly, your family's been caring for me, too. I woke up not too long before you did."

"Maybe Keely did hear me." Tobin scratched his head. "I tried asking her to help you, but I don't know if I got any words out. Where's Keely now?"

Hess's smile faded. "Back at the creek bed, maneuvering chunks of the tree bridge downstream."

Tobin's heart skipped a beat. "So, it's gone? Broken down?"

Hess nodded and glanced toward the creek. Through the gaps in the shrub line, Tobin could see the glittering water. The water that once again separated the Great Burrow from the Arakni—or what was left of them. But it separated them from something else, too. "Hess," said Tobin, "how are you going to get home?"

For a few moments, Hess just looked quietly out at the water. "I don't know."

"What about Keely?" Tobin asked.

Hess shook his head. "No, she almost drowned trying to carry me to shore. I'm a bit bulky and tend to wrap around important moving parts—like her legs and tail. I wouldn't ask her to do it again."

"Oh."

They sat in silence for a few moments. "We'll think of something."

"I know," the big snake answered.

Approaching pawsteps drew their attention. Talia and Wiley came and sat beside them, and the four friends watched the twinkling water.

"By the way." Talia broke the silence. "All the Eldermice are in a total tizzy over our story. Some are even saying we may need to revisit some of the Rules. Can you believe it?"

"Hmm." Tobin let the thought sink in a moment. "You know, I bet it's been generations since any mouse has put the Rules to the test like we did. It's probably time for review. And you should pitch your Rescue Scouts idea, too."

"Well, climb aboard," said Hess. "I'm ready to see this Great Burrow and give the elders something to really chatter about."

Wiley hopped onto Hess's back, his eyes round as cherries. "Hess, I'm really gonna like having you around."

"But not for too long," Talia added, putting a paw on Hess's side. "We'll find you a way home."

Hess nodded as she climbed onto his back. "No real hurry. I'm not sure my family, especially my mother, is quite ready to see me again."

"Hess." Tobin's mom set a paw on the serpent's cheek. "I know there's family that loves you on that side of the creek. And we'll figure out a way to get you back to them, okay?"

"Thanks." Hess nodded, and then smiled, looking to Tobin. "Want a ride?"

Tobin nodded. "But . . ." He looked at his injured tail still pressed into his side. "I don't know if I should."

"It'll be a smooth ride. Promise." Hess leaned over

and plucked him up by the scruff of his neck, setting him beside Wiley.

Wiley gently nudged him. "You know we won't let you fall."

"I know." Tobin smiled. "Just one thing." He looked toward his dad, who was now joined by his mom and baby brother, Coal. "Do you guys want a ride, too?"

His mom raised a paw. "Thanks for the offer, but I think Coal's riding days are over, at least until his eyes are open."

Tobin's dad nodded in agreement. "We'll be right behind you. And Hess." His father looked to the striped snake. "Everyone is expecting you at the Great Burrow. As long as you need it, you can call the burrow home."

Hess dipped his head in return. "Thank you."

Tobin patted the snake beneath him. Family. Eldermice. Baby news. The burrow.

Everything he'd once run from, he now happily slithered back to.

And he couldn't fight the smile.

Acknowledgments

I think Tobin would agree that when you're surrounded by supportive companions—the kind who will bravely walk an unfamiliar path with you—any journey is possible.

I'm so lucky to have had such companions. Growing up, playing on countless lakeshores with my brother, sister, and cousins, we were always encouraged to explore and be curious. To research and read and write. I had really great grown-ups in my life. Thank you, Mom and Dad and the wonderful Bellews and Wickmans.

Fast-forward a few (many) years, and the idea for a story about a brave mouse and an entire cast of creatures was born.

The idea first came while working in the field as an associate producer gathering video for South Dakota Public Broadcasting, where we did lots and lots of natural science segments. Thank you to the SDPB crew for encouraging learning, always.

Thank you to my writing group, the fabulous OWLs, for teaching me so much and starting me on the path to publication: Marlana Antifit, Jan Eldredge, José Iriarte, Lisa Iriarte, Vivi Barnes, Peggy Jackson, Jennye Kamin, Stephanie Spier, Christy Koehnlein, and Matt Tinley. Your continual support has meant the world.

Thank you to my group of publishing Super-Pros who met me on this path and led me the rest of the way: Marlo Berliner, my incredibly insightful and encouraging agent who believed in these mice from day one; Alice Jerman, editor extraordinaire with an endless supply of clever ideas, who can truly make words and stories sing; Clare Vaughn, assistant editor who provides invaluable guidance and great enthusiasm; artist Paul Scott Canavan illustrating a breathtaking cover that is truly a gateway into Tobin's world; and artist Chris Dunn for gracing the interior pages with stunning artwork that captures the mood of the story perfectly. There are no words for how grateful I am to have worked with you all.

And my family, Rob, Lily, and Izzy—thank you for staying on this journey with me. I look forward to all our adventures ahead! To my whole huge Heisel family, you are all so supportive—thank you.